Also By Shannon Esposito:

Detective Mila Harlow Series

Her Little Secret (Book 1)

The Pet Psychic Series

Karma's a Bitch

Lady Luck Runs Out

Silence Is Golden

For Pete's Sake

Pushing Up Daisies

Paws & Pose Mysteries

Faux Pas

High Jinx

Dog Gone

Frankie O'Farrell Mysteries

Buried in the Dark

Missing in the Dark

The Burning

STOLEN DAUGHTERS

A NOVEL

SHANNON ESPOSITO

misterio press

———※———

Visit Shannon Esposito's official website at:
http://murderinparadise.com

———※———

Cover Art by Dar Albert

Formatting by Debora Lewis/deboraklewis@yahoo.com

———※———

ISBN: 978-1-947287-64-8

ONE

It was the last day of a sweltering, wet summer, the sky a cloudless glazed blue. Mila Harlow leaned against the deck railing watching her ten-year-old daughter, Harper, and her best friend chuck tennis balls in the backyard for the dogs. The girls' laughter and dogs' excited yips soothed the ache in her chest.

On this day, twenty-three years ago, Mila's family had huddled around her older sister's gravestone, still shellshocked from her suicide, the cracks in their family spidering beneath the surface. Since then, her sister's birthday had become a celebration of life, a yearly remembrance, and a way to still include her in their world. A bittersweet day.

Sweat trickled down Mila's sides beneath her blue cotton sundress. She lifted a glass of ice water, pressed it against the side of her neck and leaned into the shock of cold.

Cedar-scented smoke drifted through the yard, drawing her attention to her ex-husband, Paul, who was clutching an amber beer bottle and manning the grill with her father. They were cooking the grouper for fish tacos and engaged in a conversation that had them both smiling.

A pang of jealousy stabbed her. She hadn't seen her father in months and yet they still had nothing to say to each other.

With a heaviness of heart that was becoming physical, Mila pushed herself off the railing and stepped through the sliding glass doors. The women in her family had taken over the kitchen to cook her sister's favorite foods. Conversation and laughter mingled with the TV in the living room, playing home videos of Mila, her sister and their two brothers growing up.

"Mila, here mix this for me, will ya, hon?" Her mom, Patricia, set a large bowl of eggs, brown sugar and other ingredients on the table and passed her a mixer.

"Sure." Mila wrapped her hand around the mixer handle. "Since I can see this is all you trust me with in the kitchen." She'd tried to make a joke, but it came off flat.

"Hey." Her mom squeezed her forearm. "Look at me."

Mila reluctantly met her gaze. Her mom's eyes were the same bottle green as hers but rich with hard-earned wisdom instead of pain.

"You okay? And don't lie to me."

Mila swallowed past a lump in her throat and blinked back the tears suddenly blurring her vision. She forced a smile. She didn't like to be pitied, even if it was by her own mother. "I'm fine."

"No, you're not." Her mom wrapped strong, warm arms around Mila. "You're allowed to be sad," she whispered in her ear as she rubbed her back. "You're allowed to be human."

The muscles in Mila's back and shoulders relaxed under the weight of old grief.

"What's going on over here?" Judith's silvery gaze, magnified by thick glasses, met Mila's. Being one of Mila's late grandma's best friends, she was essentially family.

"Mila just needed a hug." Her mother pulled back and winked at Mila.

Mila rolled her eyes playfully, groaned and pointed to her chest. "Grown adult. Homicide detective."

"You're never too old or too important for a hug. You know that's our specialty." Judith's halo of gray hair tickled her cheek as she wrapped soft arms around Mila.

Her grandmother's other best friend, Ruby, suddenly noticed the hug-fest and came over to join in. Her signature lemongrass and patchouli scent drifted over with her. "Whatever it is, it too shall pass."

Mila's mood lifted and she couldn't help but laugh. "Okay, okay. I love you all, too." She squeezed each of the women in her life and then extricated herself from their arms. "Get back to work now." She shooed them all back into the kitchen, where her ex-mother-in-law, Kittie, was chuckling to herself as she flipped a long, gray braid over her shoulder and pulled a pan of taco shells out of the oven.

Kittie lived with Mila and watched Harper for her while she worked. These women. They were like a web of love and support that kept Mila from hitting the ground every time she fell. She knew they would do the same for her daughter.

A swell of gratitude threatened to bring tears again.

Ugh, get a grip.

Mila concentrated on plugging in the mixer and squashing her emotions down. This was always a hard day. Her sister would've been forty-two today. Mila couldn't help but wonder... would she be married? Have kids? Become an actress like she'd dreamed about? Would their parents have stayed together without the bomb of losing Harper going off in their lives?

Mila turned her attention back to the bowl, watching the mixer whip the ingredients into a soft white cream. She just had to get through this day, then tomorrow she wouldn't feel so raw, so vulnerable and so caught off guard by sudden emotions jumping out at her from every dark corner of her psyche.

An hour later the table held a feast of Harper's favorite foods: fish tacos, Greek spinach pie, lemon and garlic potatoes, pizza with pineapple and anchovies, spiced apple, pumpkin, and lemon pies, baklava, and a chocolate birthday cake.

Mila groaned as she eyed the spread. The women in her family liked to cook a little too much. Why hadn't she got that gene? She'd be taking leftovers to the station tomorrow for sure.

They pulled chairs into the living room and held their full plates, while they watched home movies and talked about their favorite memories of Harper. Her silver-framed senior year school photo was on the coffee table beside Grandma Mary's. Ruby had placed a plate of food next to each of them.

Ruby ran a metaphysical shop out of her bed & breakfast. She didn't believe the departed ever left the people bound to them by love. Mila envied her confidence in that belief.

Harper was on the TV doing cartwheels down the beach, long dark hair flying around her smiling face, her skinny, ten-year-old frame a replica of Mila's daughter's. It was eerie that they looked so much alike, especially since Mila had named her daughter Harper to honor her sister.

Her sister had always seemed otherworldly to her. Maybe because of the story Grandma Mary had told her. The one where a two-year-old Harper had looked up from Grandma Mary's lap and declared that her sister was finally coming. Two weeks later her mom found out she was pregnant with Mila.

Another image came unbidden.

Harper at eighteen, wedged between the toilet and sink in their parents' bathroom, blood smeared all over the floor, the toilet seat, her arms, legs and face. Mila screamed. Her mom came running. Harper wouldn't stop tearing at her skin. Fresh blood seeping from her fingernails, dripping down her legs onto her feet. Her terrified voice begged them to get the bugs off her. The shrieking sirens of the ambulance.

Mila stood, her heart racing, her lungs seizing. "Excuse me," she choked out.

Dropping her still-full plate in the sink, she stepped outside on the back deck, closing her eyes and tilting her head to the sun. She stood like that for a moment, forcing deep breaths and blowing them out slowly, letting her heart rate settle back down.

"Mom? You okay?"

Mila lowered her head to see her daughter and Hannah lounging in the deck chairs with their plates of food. Their dog, Oscar, and Paul's police K-9, Max, were panting at their feet, water dripping from their jowls from a recent drink. They were all staring at her inquisitively.

She forced a smile. "Yeah, just needed some air. How's the food?"

"The fish on the pizza is kind of weird. I gave that to Oscar." Harper rubbed Oscar's back with a bare foot. "I can't believe Aunt Harper liked that." She made a disgusted face.

"So weird." Hannah pushed her frizzy blonde hair out of her eyes. "I love Grandma Kittie's pumpkin pie though." She licked the tines of her fork clean.

"Feel free to get more, Hannah. They made enough to feed an army."

"Okay, thanks." Hannah jumped off her chair and disappeared into the house.

"Mom?" Harper's voice was tentative and serious, her blue eyes watering as she squinted up into the sun.

Mila lowered herself into the deck chair next to her and waited for the question.

Harper pursed her lips, playing with the end of her dark ponytail. "Do you think Aunt Ruby's right? Like Aunt Harper is still here with us?"

Oscar licked Mila's toe and looked up at her. Comical, bushy gray brows twitched over intelligent brown eyes like he was waiting for the answer, too.

"I don't know, Harp." Mila reached over and squeezed her daughter's hand. They'd talked about death before and

Mila had been honest with her, that she just didn't know. But Harper seemed to be looking for reassurance right now. "It's possible. Do you remember the Law of Conservation of Energy?"

"Energy can neither be created or destroyed. Just changed," she recited, holding her fork up for emphasis.

"That's right. So, the energy that Aunt Harper was made of is still somewhere. It's possible she's around us, part of us." She studied her daughter's thoughtful expression. In fact, she was pretty sure whatever essence her sister was made of was the same in her daughter. A new fear snagged her heart like a fishhook. *No.* Her sister's schizophrenia was a random mutation, not hereditary. It hadn't struck anyone else down the family tree line. "You have your father's eyes," she said, knowing she was reassuring herself more than her daughter.

Harper glanced up, searching her mom's face. She didn't miss much when it came to other people's emotions. Her bare toes with chipped, sparkly pink polish were buried in Oscar's short, brown fur as her voice cracked. "So even dogs... when they die, they could stay around us?"

Mila's stomach contracted with anxiety. If she had one wish it would be to save her daughter from the pain of losing something she loved. But she knew never loving anything would be a worse fate. "Yes, even dogs."

Paul stepped out of the sliding glass doors onto the deck. Max pushed himself up, tail wagging, tennis ball clamped in his jaw. For such a fierce narcotics dog, he sure was a sucker for a ball.

Hannah appeared behind Paul. Her cheeks were pink, blonde hair frizzy and wild as she cradled a piece of pumpkin pie smothered in whipped cream.

Mila squeezed her daughter's knee then stood, giving Hannah back the chair. She smirked at the young girl. "Please don't tell your mom I let you eat that much sugar."

Hannah giggled. "Cross my heart."

Paul had stepped closer and now searched Mila's face. "You okay?"

Mila flicked her chin toward the yard. He followed her down the wooden stairs and out into the grass where they could talk privately.

Max trotted hopefully after them with the slobbery tennis ball.

Mila crossed her arms and watched as Paul chucked the tennis ball Max had dropped at his feet. The lean, three-year-old Malinois let out a sharp bark and tore through the grass after it.

An iridescent dragonfly flitted at her elbow and then swooped down toward the grass. Her sister had loved dragonflies. But she'd always told Mila if something happened to her, she'd send her a coyote mom and baby to let her know she was okay. Mila had seen a coyote twice since Harper's death but never one with a pup.

"I know today's not easy." Paul's tone was soft and empathetic, bringing her out of her thoughts. His eyes were full of sincerity and concern as they met hers, clear blue and sparkling in the sunlight.

For some reason, this stirred Mila's anger. He had no right to try and comfort her. "When were you going to tell me you're seeing someone?" She cringed inwardly. That had come out much harsher than she had practiced in her head.

Paul's expression morphed from confused to hurt. He chucked the ball across the yard again and then stared at her. "Mila, we've both been dating, right?"

Actually, no. Mila had gone on one disastrous date after their divorce five years ago and then decided it wasn't worth the hassle. But she wasn't about to admit that to Paul. "Sure, but I saw the toothbrush in your bathroom. This isn't just dating. She's staying with you." She shifted her stance in discomfort. "I don't care. It's just that I want to make sure you're not about to introduce her to Harper."

Paul's gaze darted over her face, and she knew he could see everything she was feeling, everything she wasn't saying. *The hurt. The jealousy.* "No, I'm honoring our agreement, don't worry. If there ever comes a time I'm serious enough about someone to want them to meet Harper, I'll talk to you first."

She bit the inside of her cheek, tasted the sharp tang of blood. She desperately wanted to hear him say it wasn't serious. Wanted desperately to ask him who it was. She hated feeling this out of control of her emotions. "Okay, great… thanks." She dropped her arms and turned away.

"Mila." Paul caught her hand in his, tugging her back to him.

The warmth, the familiarity of it was painful. She slowly turned to face him. "It's okay." She forced a smile, her gaze skimming his. "It's just a tough day."

He tucked her into his arms and cradled the back of her head with a palm. The way he held her was so familiar, she had the sensation of coming home. His warm breath in her ear swept away the stress. "You know I will always be here for you. No matter what happens with anyone else. You and Harper are my family."

Mila's eyes squeezed tight. *Until he remarries and starts a new family.* This thought was like a metal cage clanking down on her heart. She pulled away. "You have your own life to live. And I have mine."

Paul sighed and released her, his glance full of hurt. "Our lives are joined by Harper. You will always be my daughter's mother, and I will always care about you."

As he walked away, she had to remind herself they'd divorced for a reason. That while he made her feel alive and safe, she also felt lonely in their marriage. It was much easier to accept being lonely when you were actually alone.

As she watched him stop to talk to their daughter, her phone vibrated in her pocket. She glanced at the screen and frowned. She knew Captain Bartol wouldn't call her in today unless it was something urgent. "Captain?"

"Mila, I know today's your sister's life celebration, but we've got a body on Rattlesnake Island. A young girl." The captain paused and Mila wasn't sure if she was giving her a moment to process or herself a moment to be able to continue. "A couple of teenagers noticed the buzzards circling in the brush and found her."

"Jesus," Mila whispered, pinching the bridge of her nose. Her gaze moved to her daughter and Hannah, who were hopping down the deck stairs, jump ropes in hand. The ropes took on a sinister role in her imagination, became weapons. She had a sudden urge to tell them to go back into the house. To lock the door. There were monsters out here.

The captain's voice brought her back to the conversation. "Frank and Sergeant Lockett are on scene, along with Dr. Singh and her team. Aiden's heading to the Causeway marina now." Dr. Zansi Singh was the county medical examiner. Frank Sartori and Aiden Reyes were two detectives on their force. They had a small team, but they worked well together. "A sheriff's boat will be waiting to get you two to the island."

TWO

Mila changed into her Edgewater PD polo, black slacks, belt and holster, then retrieved her Glock from the bedroom safe. When she said her goodbyes to her family, she hugged Harper extra-long and then pulled her SUV out of the driveway.

She steered right out of her driveway onto State Road 19, the two-lane road that ran alongside the Gulf. To her left the water sparkled under the late afternoon sun, and to her right were well-manicured lawns with piles of brush and hurricane debris waiting for cleanup crews. She waved to her elderly neighbor, Bastian, as he added some palm fronds to the pile.

It had been a week since Hurricane Henry had blown through their small coastal town, leaving destruction from flooding, fallen trees and wind damage. However, things should be cleaned up by the time the snowbirds arrived next month.

Mila didn't have much time to steel herself for what she was about to see during the fifteen-minute drive to the marina. Already raw from the day, she willed herself to detach from the emotions threatening to spill over so she could do her job.

As she pulled in next to Aiden's identical white Edgewater PD SUV in the marina parking lot, she spotted the green and white sheriff's boat tied up and idling at the end of the far-left dock. Beyond the dock, the sky was cobalt blue with towers of white clouds. Too pretty a day to include a dead child.

Mila inhaled a deep breath as she walked the dock, taking in the salty air and putting aside Mila the mother, stepping into the role of Mila the homicide detective. She had learned how serial killers can compartmentalize their lives in their mind, allowing them to be husbands, fathers, and good employees. She would never understand the urge to snuff out an innocent human life, but this she understood.

"Hey." Aiden held out a hand to help her step down into the center console boat from the dock. The wind was blowing his mop of light brown hair around, his eyes hidden behind mirrored sunglasses. The hard set of his jaw was the only thing that gave away his own struggle with what they were about to see. Aiden had three little girls himself, so Mila knew he was also mentally preparing himself for this.

She shook hands with the sheriff's deputy, and then they were speeding through the light chop, the engine whining, the boat bouncing. It was only a mile to Rattlesnake Island, a crescent-moon-shaped barrier island owned by the Environmental Protection Agency of Florida. Most of the island was too primitive to explore, and it was called Rattlesnake Island for a reason. But they did allow camping and there were firepits, a few benches, and a beautiful white sand beach.

As they approached, she could see three other law enforcement boats anchored close to shore, along with a couple of kayaks pulled up on the sand. Four uniformed officers were conducting a search around the narrow beach. Mila glanced back toward the coastline. No homes close enough to witness the body dump. Some mansions along the beach across the way, and a bigger island accessible by the Edgewater Causeway two miles to the south. No sight or sound witnesses. No cameras. This one was going to be a nightmare to solve.

The deputy maneuvered the twenty-six-foot Yellowfin as close to shore as possible without getting it stuck in the sand. He glanced at the detectives as he raised the engine and tossed the anchor overboard. "May want to remove your shoes to get out."

Mila and Aiden took his suggestion, rolling up their pants and holding their black athletic oxfords and leather binders as they landed in the warm, calve-deep water and made their way to shore. Once there, they dusted the damp sand off their feet as best they could and leaned on each other to put their socks and shoes back on. Then they headed toward Sergeant Lockett and Officer Meyers.

Sergeant Lockett was standing in front of yellow crime scene tape staked at the entrance of a narrow path leading into the brush. His hands rested on his duty belt, his bald, brown head shiny with sweat, and puffy dark patches beneath his eyes.

"Detectives," he greeted them bleakly and pointed down the beach. "Officers Gentry and Simms have separated the complainants. Two young men found her. A seventeen- and eighteen-year-old. They kayaked here to fish and saw the buzzards." He took out a white handkerchief and wiped the sweat from his brow, indicating the path behind him with a jerk of his thumb. "That's the only path leading to the victim. Zansi's team has already searched it for any evidence. Besides a few rusty beer cans, they got zip. They've moved on to process the body. Frank did the walk-through with them and is still back there." Then he gestured to a box in the sand. "They left you some PPE. Brace yourselves. It's a bad one."

She and Aiden shared a glance.

"I'll talk to Gentry, Simms and the kids, then catch up with you," Aiden said.

Mila nodded, grabbed the protective equipment including paper booties and N-95 mask, and shoved a pair of gloves into her pocket. Then she ducked under the crime scene tape and signed the log on Officer Myers's clipboard. He was a rookie, about eighteen months in, and his pale, sweaty complexion looked like he might be reexamining his life choices.

"Just follow the smell," he said ominously. "And watch your step."

She moved down the narrow path. It was mushy beneath her steps and blanketed by fallen brown pine needles. The island was still saturated from the storm last week, so there were puddles to avoid. She also watched out for rattlers crossing her path as she pushed the overgrown brush out of her way. So far there had only been a scattering of lizards and a chattering squirrel.

Deep inside the overgrown brush felt like a sauna. Sweat gathered around her hairline and trickled down the back of her neck. Her chest was tight and her breathing labored. She dreaded putting on the mask and making it worse.

With each step, she tried to put herself in the perp's shoes.

How did the killer carry a body through here? How did they even find this place?

She quickly got close enough to the site for the unmistakable smell of death to hit her in the face. It seeped into her nose and clawed its way down her throat. With a gagging cough, she slipped on the mask and gloves and then broke through the brush into a small clearing.

Within a square of red crime scene tape, three people in white Tyvek suits worked around the body on the ground. The ME's office had its own crime scene investigators, who Edgewater PD called to work big cases like homicides.

A camera flash popped off.

Mila spotted the medical examiner, Dr. Zansi Singh, kneeling near the body. Her Tyvek suit hid her small frame and long, dark hair.

The low drone of a vacuum mingled with various island birds screeching their warnings about the human invaders.

Frank stood on the other side of the red crime scene tape, masked, his head bowed, his notebook tucked under one arm. Misa made her way over to him. "I'm assuming there was no ID on the body."

"There's not even a face." His voice was muffled by the mask, but his frustration was still clear. Sweat rolled down his sideburns and neck as he glanced around the area. "I'm going to do another walk-around. Make sure we didn't miss anything." He pointed around the backside of the crime scene tape. "You can enter back there to talk to the doc."

Mila nodded, waved a hand in front of her face to chase off a swarm of mosquitoes and moved in that direction. She watched P.J. O'Malley, one of the ME techs, squatting and wielding a small hand vacuum, which she scanned deliberately over the body. That was something Mila hadn't seen before.

Opening her leather binder to a new sheet of steno paper, she jotted down notes, drew a rough sketch of how the body was positioned. Then she waited for Dr. Zansi Singh to wave her over and ducked under the crime scene tape.

Mila's legs were tingling and stiff from standing in one place by the time Zansi stood to greet her, her voice muffled by her mask. She was a small woman with a big presence. "Sorry you had to come in today." Her dark brown eyes were glowing with compassion. She knew today was Mila's sister's yearly celebration of life. It was a small town and law enforcement was a tight-knit community. "Especially for this."

"Thanks. What do we know so far?"

Zansi cocked her head and moved her attention back to the body. "Not much. Young female. She's got some canine teeth erupting, so I'd estimate her age somewhere in the ballpark of nine, maybe ten."

Mila cringed. *The same age as Harper.* "Cause of death?"

She shook her head. "Don't know yet."

Mila made herself study the body. It was bloated, flesh marbled green and black. Some skin had slipped off the corpse. The eye sockets were empty, probably fed on by buzzards or crows rather than mutilation by the killer. Triangle-shaped wounds on her face and neck from scavenger birds supported this theory. The girl had on a ruffled pink dress, torn and dirty, no shoes. But something else was missing.

Mila narrowed her eyes, thinking about the other bodies she'd observed. Then she got it. "No flies?" she asked.

"Good question. And the answer is ants." She pointed to P.J. O'Malley. "She's vacuuming up the colony, but they ate the fly eggs and larvae. They've been here long enough to feed on the body, also, creating lesions that they've progressively torn skin from. Without the flies, the rate of decay is affected. So, along with the hot, wet environment which speeds up decomp, it's going to be harder to estimate time of death."

Mila took a step closer and stared at an item lying a few inches from the long blonde stands of hair still attached to the scalp, which had slipped partially from the skull.

A plastic silver birthday crown with pink stones glued to it.

Did she die on her birthday?

The party dress seemed to indicate so, though Mila didn't see any shoes around. "She was definitely dumped here after the hurricane. This island got flooded so that," Mila gestured with her pen toward the birthday crown, "would have washed away from the body."

"Agree," Dr. Singh said. "And there is some saponification happening, so that would fit the week timeline. But I need to get her back to the morgue to be sure."

The sound of the vacuum went silent as P.J. stood and moved away from the body, throwing Dr. Singh a thumbs-up sign.

"Tragic. I wonder who she is," Mila said quietly.

"Well, the only missing girl from this area we know about is Amelia Larson. The little girl who disappeared three years ago. She wasn't this old, though."

"No, she was only six," Mila said. One year younger than Harper when she'd gone missing. The paralyzing panic Mila had felt had been out of proportion to the threat to Harper. That hadn't stopped her from keeping Harper indoors for a week. Her deepest fear was not being able to keep her daughter safe, and not even a professional counselor could convince her it was irrational. It had been the reason they'd adopted Oscar, and Paul had trained him as a guard dog.

"You think you can get fingerprints?" Mila stared at the paper bags they'd placed over the dead girl's decayed hands. "DNA will take too long."

"There is skin slippage, but I can maybe work with that. Hopefully, she's in the system. I can tell you one thing." Zansi kneeled and pointed to the left side of the body with a gloved finger. "See this darker skin, the lividity along her shoulder, hip and calf? She died on her side, was there for up to twelve hours before being moved. There are no obvious signs of trauma. No gunshot wounds, stab wounds. It's possible I'll find something during the autopsy, but right now I have no idea how she died."

Mila let her gaze wander around the area. Frank was walking along the south edge of the brush. "She was moved here, not killed here. I suppose she could have died accidentally. Someone panicked and dumped her body instead of reporting it. Still, a strange place to dump a body. It would have to be a local who knew this place."

"Seems like it."

They both turned to watch a second ME crime tech, Brooklyn, gently slip the crown into a large brown paper bag and label it. Mila frowned. "Why leave the birthday crown with her though? You'd think whoever did this would want to minimize evidence. They had to know there could be fingerprints or DNA on that crown."

"They probably panicked. Weren't thinking straight," Zansi answered. "Or if it was someone unfamiliar with forensics, leaving evidence wouldn't even cross their mind."

"Could be." Mila tapped her notebook against her thigh as she thought. "Or that crown meant something to the girl. They felt guilty, didn't want her to be without it." A welcomed breeze stirred the hair on Mila's shoulders. The sun was dropping in the sky. "This island is only accessible by boat, so whoever dumped her here had to have access to one." She took a few steps back. "Can't do much about people who own boats but when we know an approximate time frame, we can check boat rentals."

Zansi nodded. "I'll be performing the autopsy at 8 AM if you want to be present."

The thump thump of a helicopter approaching made them glance up. It was coming in fast, quickly eating up the distance and dipping low to get closer to the island.

"The press." Zansi cursed. "I should've put up the tent. Just thought a remote island would take them longer to get to." She turned to her team. "Let's get the body bagged ASAP."

Mila peeled off the gloves as she watched the helicopter settling above them like a giant cockroach. Social media was becoming a huge problem. She knew there were multiple Facebook pages where people posted any sightings of police or police activity in Edgewater. They were becoming more of an issue than the folks who listened to their radio comms. Law Enforcement was careful to use cell phones for big cases like this, but you couldn't stop people from noticing police activity. Citizen journalism was a plague.

"I'll see you in the morning." Hopefully for some kind of lead.

Back at the station, Mila and Aiden searched every database they had access to for a missing girl, ages eight to twelve, who fit the description. It was frustrating. Until they had an ID on their victim, there wasn't much they could do.

Dr. Singh would run fingerprints—if she could get them. If nothing popped, she'd send an X-ray of the victim's jaw and teeth through NamUs, the National Missing and Unidentified Persons system. Though if this girl has only been dead for a week, she may not have even been added to the system yet.

Until then, Mila logged onto the Law Enforcement Enterprise portal, giving her access to VICAP, the Violent Criminals Apprehension Program. It was an FBI database with information on national homicide and assault cases. Mila searched for homicides involving young girls with "birthday" and "crown" as keywords. No hits. This was just an initial search though she would try again when they had a cause of death or any other major criteria.

Captain Bartol burst from her office, a scowl on her face. Her pixie cut was freshly dyed red, covering the gray that had begun to show. Her curvy figure was clad in black slacks and a pale green blouse. She'd been Captain of the Investigative Division for eight years now and was well respected by the community she'd called home for the last thirty years. Mila found her to be tough but fair.

"The news is all over this. Elly Prescott's broadcasting live from the marina. What is she, psychic?" she grumbled.

"She could be monitoring social media," Mila offered.

The captain stood next to Mila's desk and massaged her forehead roughly. "They've got footage of the body bag being loaded onto the boat and know it was a young female. Did that come from the two witnesses?"

"Nope," Aiden answered. "They were escorted back to shore by the sheriff's deputy, with threat of jail for impeding an investigation if they talked to the press."

She nodded her approval. "We've got to find that damn leak."

Mila blew out a breath. "Yeah, she could've only learned it's a young girl from one of our own."

Elly Prescott was a hungry young reporter who knew how to use her beauty to get a story and didn't care who she hurt in the process. Mila pushed back from the computer and rubbed at her dry, blurry eyes. "Seems like they know as much as we do."

"Nothing in the databases then?" Captain Bartol asked.

Mila shook her head and looked at Aiden. "You got anything?"

"Nada." He looked as defeated as she felt. "We have no witnesses, no ID, nowhere to start."

Captain Bartol stared at the monitor. "All right. Go get a few hours of sleep. Frank and Matt are going to stay tonight in case any leads come in. Hopefully, the autopsy will give you two a jumping-off point in the morning. You can both attend."

⁕

The autopsy was scheduled too early for Mila to drive Harper to school, so she'd planted a kiss on her sleeping daughter's warm cheek and left the drive to Kittie. Since the morgue was in the opposite direction of her mom's coffee shop, she settled for grabbing the thick, bitter brew at Gasmart on the way.

By the time she rolled into the gravel parking lot of the tan two-story building that held the morgue and forensics lab, she felt awake, but the dull pull of sleepiness had been replaced by a hard pit of dread in her stomach.

She shut the driver's door and began mentally preparing for the autopsy. The sound of tires crunching on the gravel got her attention. Aiden was pulling in behind her.

As he approached, Mila eyed the bags under his eyes, knowing he hadn't slept much either. "Morning. Ready for this?"

"Never." He sighed as they walked to the building and opened the glass door for her.

"Detectives." Carmen, the thirty-something Latino woman behind the bulletproof window, greeted them. She slid the plastic guest badges through the opening, anger burning in her eyes. "I hope you catch this bastard."

Mila nodded, noticing Carmen looked much more rested than the last time she was here. Her new baby boy must be sleeping better. "We'll do our best."

"I got faith in you," Carmen said, buzzing them into the main hallway.

Their rubber-soled shoes squeaked on the freshly scrubbed linoleum floors as they walked side by side to the electric doors that slid open, granting them entrance into the morgue.

Mila could already taste the formaldehyde and stench of death on her tongue as she reached into a box on the shelf to her right and pulled out two masks, handing one to Aiden.

"Morning, Detectives." Zansi greeted them clad in a blue surgical gown, gloves, and both a mask and plastic face shield. She stood on the other side of the metal pedestal table that held the girl's body.

Her assistant, Lonnie, was dressed the same as she worked beside her boss.

Lonnie's dark brown eyes flicked up to greet them. "Good morning." Then she went back to the grueling work of bending over the body with a camera, photographing the lesions on the black and bloated face and neck.

They stepped forward and stood across from the two women. Mila's gaze dropped to the table. Strands of scraggly blonde hair were still attached to the scalp. The victim's tongue was protruding from her blackened lips. If she didn't know better, she'd think this girl was a burn victim.

Mila choked back bile as she imagined Harper on this cold metal table. She squeezed her eyes shut for a brief moment, getting her thoughts under control, and putting up the wall between her personal and work life.

When she opened them, Zansi's warm chestnut eyes were assessing her behind the shield. She missed nothing.

Mila nodded that she was okay.

Zansi once again gave the victim her attention. "After a cursory check, I still don't see a cause of death. X-rays don't show any broken bones, current or in her history, so she wasn't abused. It may be some type of asphyxia... manual strangulation, choking, or suffocation, but with this level of decomp, it's difficult to say. Unfortunately, postmortem toxicology cannot detect raised levels of carbon dioxide. We may get lucky and find nasal bone fractures or inhaled fibers, but I'm not holding my breath." She looked up at them.

Mila digested all that and then said, "I think the most important thing right now is to get an ID." She checked with Aiden, who nodded in agreement.

Zansi shared a glance with Lonnie, who nodded. "We can surely try."

Lonnie carefully removed the paper bag from the right hand of the victim, taking a closeup photo of each fingertip before she placed her camera on the counter. When she returned to the body, she and Zansi worked together to detach the already loosened skin from the right hand, slipping it off like a glove.

Mila and Aiden watched in both horror and fascination as Lonnie helped fit the dead girl's skin over Zansi's petite gloved hand, making sure the delicate fingertips didn't tear. At one point, Mila had to remind herself to breathe. Lonnie then slowly inked and rolled the prints on a card.

Zansi nodded in satisfaction as they stared at the results. "Lonnie, go ahead and take this over to Gwynn to run through AFIS," she said. "See if she can put a rush on getting us a name."

Mila knew Gwynn was one of their latent print examiners. "Thanks," she said. "Let us know if there's a hit."

Back at the station Mila sat at her desk, haunted by images of the girl wearing a birthday crown, dumped on Rattlesnake Island. Just like her sister, the little girl would never have another birthday, never get to fulfill her dreams, fall in love, have a family, or have a career. The injustice of a life cut short made her dizzy with rage. She would never understand how someone could kill a child. Someone obviously cared enough about her to give her a pretty dress and birthday crown.

Maybe it was an accident. Still. Why hide the body on a remote island where it wasn't likely to be found? Why leave the girl alone to be consumed by nature instead of a proper burial?

A wave of nausea washed over her. She checked the time and pushed away from her desk. It was almost lunchtime, and she'd dumped way too much coffee into her stomach with no food. She was just about to ask Aiden if he wanted to grab some lunch when her desk phone rang.

She snatched up the receiver, her heart racing when she saw the number on caller ID. "Tell me you have something."

"I have something," Zansi said. "Are you sitting down?"

THREE

Mila was staring at Aiden, who had turned around in his chair when she answered the call. He was watching her expectantly, arms crossed.

"Are you sure?" Mila croaked. "I mean. Of course, you're sure but how..." She shook her head. "Sorry, just processing. Okay, thank you." She hung up and blinked at Aiden.

"Who is it?" he asked.

Her heartbeat thumped like a drum in her ears as she choked out, "Amelia Larson." She watched as the same confusion played out on his face. The same thoughts. Eighty-nine percent of kidnapping victims are murdered within the first twenty-four hours. Obviously not the case here.

"But she was six." It hit him. His face paled. "Oh, God. Someone's been keeping her alive all this time." He leaned back in his chair and blew out a breath. After a few moments, his troubled eyes focused back on her. "It's a miracle her prints were on file."

Mila nodded and then went to her computer to look up Amelia's next of kin. As she opened the file, she explained, "Remember how Florida gave out those free in-home fingerprinting kits to schools? Well, Amelia's mother actually used it and turned it over to Crystal Harbor PD when her daughter went missing."

Pushing aside horrifying thoughts, thoughts of what might have happened to the little girl in the last three years, she picked up her phone. She'd already called Crystal Harbor

PD to get the girl's case file, but for now, she needed to notify the family before the leak in the department gave the press Amelia's name. Pushing a hand against her protesting stomach to quiet it, she met Aiden's gaze. "Want to come with me to tell the mother?"

"Not really. But I will." He stood, stretched his lower back and then sighed. "I'll go fill in the captain. Meet you outside."

They took Mila's SUV and headed north on US 19. The two-lane road followed the coast for a few miles then curved inland, taking them past rundown diners, bait shops, a smattering of houses and seedy motels. Traffic was heavy, but Mila wasn't in a hurry to break the news to Amelia's mother.

Eventually, the drive turned more esthetically pleasing with newer buildings and rows of palm trees planted along the roadway. They passed the large, bright blue wooden sign welcoming them to the town of Crystal Harbor where Amelia Larson had lived her short life.

Mila followed the GPS to the northeast side of town, where the cute beach shops, restaurants and strip malls gave way to dollar stores, pawn shops, and laundromats. They turned into Sunshine Trailer Park, and Mila's jaw clenched. She couldn't imagine being on the other end of this news.

Stop. Don't imagine.

But she had. A million times. She couldn't stop imagining.

"This is it," she said, as they pulled up to a white trailer with a candy-striped red and white awning. Large clay pots with pink and white Petunias sat on either side of the small concrete patio. A flock of white Ibis poked their curved orange beaks into the sandy yard. The birds hurried to the next yard as Mila and Aiden knocked on the aluminum screen door. The scent of Mexican food drifted from inside and Mila fought another wave of nausea. God, she hated this part of the job.

A bone-thin woman in an oversized Bud Light T-shirt and green leggings materialized behind the screen. "Yes?" Her tone was suspicious and unfriendly. Her face etched with grief like water etches rock over time.

"Bobby Sue Larson?" Mila asked, holding up her badge. "I'm Detective Harlow and this is Detective Reyes. May we come in? We have some news about Amelia."

Bobby Sue fell forward, shoving the screen door open. Soft brown eyes were now filled with hope. "Come in." She waved a bony, frantic arm.

They followed her inside the tidy living room with worn, flowered furniture. Photos of Amelia at all ages were hung on the wall behind the sofa. One in particular caught Mila's eye.

Amelia must've been around three, blonde hair curling around her earlobes, her tiny arms wrapped around a tabby cat. Mila had a similar photo of Harper with the neighbor's cat.

Turning away, she lowered herself on the sofa next to Aiden. A large canvas painting above the TV grabbed her attention next. Mila openly stared. It was extraordinary. Obviously Amelia, but she was wearing a princess gown and set in some kind of fantasy world, blonde hair glowing, wide smile, sparkling eyes caught mid-joy. The extravagant painting seemed out of place in this small trailer.

"Did you find her? Did you find my baby?" Bobby Sue's shaky voice asked. Her hands were clutched together so hard, her knuckles were turning white.

Mila pulled her gaze away from the painting and gave Bobby Sue the full attention she deserved. "I'm afraid we did, Ms. Larson. I'm so sorry, but her body was found on Rattlesnake Island yesterday. We identified her through fingerprints at the autopsy this morning."

Mila gave her a moment to process the news. She felt numb, detached from the moment like she was watching the woman fall apart from far away.

"Oh, God. Oh no." Bobby Sue rocked forward, hanging her head between her knees. She wept quietly. After a while, she lifted her head and snatched a Kleenex from the coffee table. Her eyes were shiny with grief and shock, her face blotchy. "What happened to her?"

Aiden kept his tone quiet and respectful as he delivered even more devastating news. "The autopsy was inconclusive on cause of death. I can tell you that she was kept alive until about a week ago."

Bobby Sue's head snapped up. Horror filled her gaze. "Alive?" Her pupils dilatated behind a sheen of tears. "What did the bastard do to her for three years?" The tears broke free and rolled down her face. She covered her mouth with a shaking hand.

After a respectful few moments, Aiden spoke gently. "We'd like to ask you a few questions if you're up for it."

Bobby Sue dropped her hand and nodded, but her gaze was focused on the table, pupils large and black as night. She was in shock.

Mila leaned forward to get in her line of sight. "Ms. Larson, we're going to get the case file, but I'd like to hear in your own words if there was anyone you suspected of Amelia's abduction when it happened?"

There was suddenly a cold fire in her eyes as her nostrils flared. "Cole." She said the name like she was spitting. "Cole Richards. He was my boyfriend of two years. Before Amelia disappeared, there was an incident. He was drunk, thought I'd stepped out on him. He was screeching and yelling one night, waving a gun around, talking about I need to remember who I belong to." Her jaw clenched. "He got to be a crazy bastard when he got on the Jack Daniels. Anyway, the gun went off. Straight through the bedroom wall and grazed Amelia's arm while she was in bed." Bobby Sue's fists were clenched as she recalled the memory. "I rushed her to the ER, despite him begging me to just bandage it up at home. There was just so much blood. Of course, the doctor called the cops, and Cole was arrested. He wasn't supposed to have a firearm. Never forgave me. He just got out two weeks ago. I've already got a bunch of harassing phone calls from him."

Mila and Aiden shared a glance. Then Aiden said, "But if he got out two weeks ago, he couldn't have been holding Amelia all this time."

"True." A pained expression crossed her face. "But his brother could've."

Mila clicked her pen open. "What's his brother's name?"

"Garrett Levington. Thick as thieves, even though they got different daddies. Real piece of work, that one. Lives up in Odessa. He'd have done it if Cole asked him to. Taken Amelia for revenge." A sob tore from her throat. "To hurt me cause I let him go to jail. I told the detective about him... Detective Scott was the fellow's name. He did talk to Garrett; said he had an alibi. But you know what? He'd have no problem threatenin' someone to lie for him."

"Would you mind showing us Amelia's room? I'd like to recheck to make sure the first investigators didn't miss anything," Mila said.

Bobby Sue stood, bracing herself on the back of the chair. "Her room is just the way she left it."

She led them to the second door on the right. Her hand shook as she turned the doorknob and let the door swing open. As they stepped in to search the bedroom, she turned away.

A layer of dust had settled over the things on her dresser. Mila carefully opened a jewelry box, sifting through the plastic costume jewelry with a gloved hand. Nothing of consequence. Aiden had pushed aside the clothes in the closet and was kneeling, looking inside a box in the corner.

"Anything?" Mila asked as she stood up from searching beneath the bed and mattress.

"Nope. No secrets here."

"All right, let's get out of here."

They stepped back into the living room, where Bobby Sue sat back in the chair, looking lost.

"One more thing. When was Amelia's birthday?" Mila asked.

"February sixth." Her eyes drifted to the photos on the wall behind the detectives, and her body began to tremble. "I tried to hold on, tried to believe she'd come home. She was such a sweet girl." She choked back a sob. "You'll let me know when you find out who done this?"

Mila and Aiden both nodded. Then Mila handed her a card. "We will. The medical examiner will be calling you soon to release your daughter's body, but you can call me anytime if you need an update on our investigation. Again, we're so sorry for your loss."

As they walked out, a white Toyota Corolla was parking in front of the mailbox. The small, blonde woman who stepped out of the car waved.

Mila waited for her to reach them before saying, "Hey, Jenny. You got here quick."

Jenny Benderson was a civilian victim advocate trained by the sheriff's department. Mila had worked with her to get a restraining order for one of the women they'd lost to domestic violence a few years back. The restraining order had been granted, but it ultimately didn't stop the bullet that took the woman's life.

Jenny clutched a large book bag beneath one armpit and nodded at them. "I was in the area when Captain Bartol reached me. She said it was this woman's daughter you found on Rattlesnake Island?"

"Yeah. Amelia Larson. She was six when she went missing three years ago. Looks like she's been dead about a week."

"Horrible." Jenny's mouth pinched but she straightened her petite shoulders. "Crisis management it is."

"Also, give her a head's up that the press will come knocking. Good luck," Mila said, hopping up into the SUV.

She watched Jenny rap on the door and Bobby Sue motion her in, while Aiden looked up both Cole and Garrett in the database. "It wasn't anywhere near Amelia's birthday. So why the birthday crown?" Mila asked quietly.

"I don't know about that," Aiden said. "But she's right. Cole did a three-year stint for aggravated child abuse, using a firearm while under the influence of alcohol, child endangerment and culpable negligence. He was released two weeks ago." He studied the terminal mounted between them. "And Garrett's got a few priors for burglary and sexual assault. Nothing in the last three years."

"Keeping his nose clean." Mila glanced over at him with concern. When they got the full autopsy report, they would know if Amelia had been sexually assaulted. "So, if Garrett was holding Amelia while his brother was in prison, Cole could've decided to get rid of the girl now that he's out."

She bit the inside of her cheek, thinking. "Maybe he didn't want his brother keeping her alive but couldn't do anything about it until he was out." It was a horrific thought, but one she had to consider. Mila backed out of the driveway, reminding herself to unclench her jaw.

"We need to talk to both of them." Aiden's voice was raspy with unspoken anger.

As they drove back down the main road, the car in front of them crept up to the red light and she followed suit. But she wasn't seeing the road or the car. Against her will, her mind was rehashing all the stories of the girls who had made it home after a long abduction.

What had it cost them? How many could sleep without waking up screaming from nightmares, horrible memories of the things that happened to them? How many were too damaged to trust again? To have normal relationships? To live without terror and pain?

"Maybe it's better she is at peace now," she said, though she didn't mean to say it out loud.

A long sigh came from Aiden. "There are worse things than death."

Back at the station, they found Frank standing in the bullpen talking to Captain Bartol.

"Hey." Mila took in his pale complexion and thinner frame. Something was going on with him other than staying up last night. She was beginning to believe he was either sick or his pending divorce was taking a toll on him. "Got anything?"

"Nada," Frank said. His eyes looked sunken behind dark-framed glasses.

"What about you two?" Captain Bartol asked, eyeing Frank like she was thinking about sending him home. She shifted off her bad knee. "You get anything from the mother to follow up on?"

"Yeah," Mila said. "Apparently there was an incident with her ex, Cole Richards, right before Amelia disappeared. He accidentally shot the little girl while drunk, went to prison for it. Just got released two weeks ago." She held up her hand when she saw the same question forming in the captain's eyes. "He has a brother in Odessa." She checked her notes. "Garrett Levington. Bobby Sue thinks he would've taken Amelia for the brother. She said he had an alibi at the time of the abduction, but we'll have to recheck that."

"So, we're thinking it's possible Cole Richards didn't want the brother keeping Amelia alive, gets out of prison and takes care of her himself." Aiden rested his hands on his hips casually, but the tension in his jaw and shoulders gave away the anger he was struggling with.

Captain Bartol's expression tensed, and she suddenly looked nauseous as the implication of the brother holding

Amelia for three years hit. She cleared her throat, but it still held a deep rasp. "Okay, Aiden, you take a drive out to Odessa and have a conversation with Garrett Levington. Frank, you see if you can find Cole Richards." She turned to Mila. "The files have arrived from Crystal Harbor PD. I had them dropped by your desk. Find us something they missed."

"Yes, ma'am." Mila nodded at her teammates, silently hoping she could obey that order.

FOUR

Mila went to the breakroom and grabbed peanut butter crackers and an apple juice to keep her stomach from interrupting her for now. There were three brown Bekins boxes stacked beside her desk, Amelia's name and case number on the labels. Dropping her snack beside her computer monitor, she settled into her desk chair and pulled the lid off the top box. She lifted out the first three-ring binder and began to read, reminding herself to keep an open mind, to look at this abduction as if it had just happened, not as if she already knew the grim outcome.

Amelia Larson disappeared three years ago on February 24th from the Safety Harbor Seafood Festival. She'd been there with her mother, Bobby Sue Larson. According to the mother, she'd been talking to a friend she'd run into, Shelby Myers, and when they parted ways, she couldn't find Amelia.

Mila made a note to look up the interview with Shelby Myers then pulled up the address for the festival on her computer, along with a map. She typed in "Veterans Memorial Park in Safety Harbor." It was on the east coast of the peninsula, off Old Tampa Bay.

Whoever dumped Amelia's body on Rattlesnake Island had to have used a boat. Did they use a boat to abduct her, too? How did the kidnapper know she would be at that festival? Was it just a crime of opportunity? That would be worst-case scenario because then there would be no connections between the girl and the kidnapper to help them find him.

She jotted down those questions in her notebook and then continued to read through the binder. She skipped through the canvas for now, skipped the vehicle information noted around the area, witness statements, background checks. Right now she wanted to know if they had any suspects or hard evidence.

Coming across the file on Garrett Levington, the boyfriend's brother, she pulled out the interview notes. She'd want to watch the full interview later, but for now she was looking for his alibi. After a brief read-through, she found it. Brenda Creedy. Girlfriend. She jotted down the name to reinterview her. Maybe she was now an ex-girlfriend and willing to fess up if she'd lied for him.

Mila spent the next three hours going through the rest of the case files. When she felt her blood sugar drop in the form of a dizzy spell, she reluctantly replaced the lid on the second box and popped the last cracker into her mouth. She checked her notes as she chewed.

The only significant lead she had to follow up on was Brenda Creedy. What she really needed to do was talk to the lead detective on the case, Detective Logan Scott. Even cold cases are still worked when the lead detective has time. Maybe he has a new theory or new suspect. She looked up the number for Crystal Harbor PD and left him a message.

She also found a number for Brenda Creedy and left her a message to please return her call.

The scent of Chinese food suddenly made her mouth water. Great, she was so hungry, she was hallucinating.

"I assume you haven't eaten," Aiden said, holding up a white plastic bag.

"I should be offended by your assumption." She grinned up at him. "But I'm too hungry to be anything but grateful. Thanks."

Aiden sat in his chair and turned it around to face her desk while she unsealed the plastic cover from the shrimp and veggie dish, releasing the heavenly aroma. Her stomach gurgled in response. Aiden unwrapped a spring roll and took a bite.

After he swallowed, he said, "I finally found Garrett Levington at a local car shop in Odessa where he works. Wouldn't say he was the most cooperative fella." His brows raised under his mop of wavy hair and Mila knew that was an understatement. "He also wouldn't say if he's seen his brother since his release. I did take a peek around his property, though and he's got a bit of land and a shed. Could've hidden the girl in there. If we can disprove his alibi, we may be able to get a warrant to search the place."

Mila nodded as she swallowed a bite of shrimp and rice, feeling her stomach cramp with the first real food all day. "His alibi was a girlfriend, Brenda Creedy. I've left her a message. If she doesn't return my call today, let's go find her. I also left a message for Detective Logan Scott. He was the lead on Amelia's disappearance." She took a few more bites, feeling her energy return. "Have you heard anything from Frank yet?"

Aiden wiped his fingers on a napkin and checked his phone. "Nothing yet."

"Have you noticed he hasn't been looking too good lately? He's always popping Tums and isn't drinking coffee anymore. Maybe he's got an ulcer. You think the divorce is getting to him?" Going through one divorce was hard enough, but this was his third failed marriage and Lenore was a spitfire. She was fighting for the house, even though it had been Frank's when they met.

Aiden blinked, his gaze not quite reaching hers. "Possible."

Mila tilted her head. "You know something." Aiden was great at lying to suspects to get information, but terrible at lying to people he cared about. "Spill."

He leaned back in his chair and blew out a long breath. "I can't. Honestly, I think he just needed someone to confide in. But he asked me not to say anything so…" he shrugged helplessly.

"Can you just tell me if it's serious?"

His head bobbed around in a yes and no.

"Is he dying?"

Aiden rubbed at the gold stubble on his cheek. "No, not anytime soon."

Mila was satisfied with that. As she washed down a bite with the last sip of apple juice, her desk phone rang. She snatched up the receiver. "Detective Harlow." She coughed, almost choking on the shrimp she hadn't quite gotten down. "Sorry, hello?"

"Hi, this is Brenda. You left a message that you needed to talk to me about something urgent. By the way, it's Brenda Gorski now. Got hitched last year."

Mila gave a thumbs up to Aiden as she said, "Yes, thanks for returning my call, Mrs. Gorski. Actually, I'd like to discuss it in person if you don't mind." It was much easier to tell if someone was lying face to face. She heard the hesitation in the sudden silence on the other end of the phone. "I can come to you."

"Well, um… I'm just on a smoke break right now and have to get back to work."

"Where do you work?"

"The Rat's Nest in Crystal Harbor. Off Channel Street. I work the bar."

"Be there in twenty minutes." She hung up to keep any protests at bay. As she gathered her keys, phone and notebook, shoving them into her leather satchel, she glanced at Aiden. "Go ahead and work on that search warrant for

Garrett Levington's place. Brenda Creedy is now Brenda Gorski. She got married to someone else. I've got a good feeling about this."

※

The Rat's Nest was at the end of a dilapidated strip mall, sandwiched between a Dollar General and Bill's Laundromat. A few Harleys and muscle cars sat in the parking lot. The front windows of the building were tinted black. On the door was a large, stenciled rat, wearing a leather vest and motorcycle helmet and holding a frothing mug of beer. Mila's hand moved to her holster beneath her blazer to ensure her Glock was in place. These would not be the type of people to trust law enforcement.

When she opened the door, she was hit with icy air and the smell of fried food, cheap cologne and body odor. Quickly scanning the small, dim room she clocked twelve guys and three women. One couple at the pool table. All their eyes were locked on her in curious but unwelcoming stares.

Ignoring them, she made her way to the right side of the bar as all the men were congregated to the left so they could watch the NASCAR race playing on the TV above them.

A busty redhead with a raised scar above her eyebrow and a black and white skull with butterfly wings tattooed on her throat hustled over. "What can I getcha?" Her tone wasn't friendly. She flipped the bar towel over her shoulder and shook her head slightly.

Mila got the message. *Not here.* "Just need a Diet Coke… to go."

"To go. Good idea," she announced loudly, presumably so the men down the bar, who were openly eyeballing Mila, could hear.

Mila stared back until they got uncomfortable and looked away.

Brenda returned with a Styrofoam drink, took Mila's money and then slipped her a note with the change. "Have a nice day."

Mila gave a little wave to her fan club as she strolled back to the door. Once outside, she unfolded the note and read: *Meet me out back in 5*

She walked around the side of the building to the back, where two plastic chairs were set up, an ashtray on the ground between them. She took a seat in one of the chairs and sipped on her Diet Coke. There was no shade back here and no breeze. The heat immediately gathered beneath her armpits and the back of her neck. She removed her blazer and draped it over the back of the chair while staying alert to the sound of any footsteps coming her way.

Fifteen minutes crept by. Mila began wondering if she should go in for a refill when Brenda stuck her head out the back door. She looked disappointed Mila was still there. Glancing once more behind her, she emerged and lowered herself into the second chair, lighting a cigarette. "I only got a few minutes. So what can I help you with?"

She'd get right to it then. "Do you remember a little girl who went missing three years ago? Amelia Larson?"

Brenda's eyes fluttered closed for a moment. "Yes." The word came out soft on a wave of gray smoke.

"You gave an alibi for your boyfriend, Garrett Levington, at the time. Said he was with you fishing the day she disappeared." Mila watched the emotion shift her facial features until her mouth was pinched with guilt, making the smoker's wrinkles prominent.

She glanced over at Mila, her shoulders stiffening. "I did."

Mila had to be very careful here. "You're not in any trouble. People lie for their loved ones for lots of reasons. But it's important, if you did lie for him, that you tell me the truth now."

She lifted her hand and stared at the smoke coming off her cigarette. "I got to babysit for Amelia once, you know. When her mom was in a pinch with work. We was in town, and I could tell she didn't really want to leave her with me. Hell, she didn't know me from Adam. But Cole vouched for me, said I was great with kids." She scoffed. "Like he would know. Anyway, she was the sweetest little thing. We played Barbies and did a puzzle. Bobby Sue... she was a good mom. I can't imagine the pain she went through." She sniffed and wiped her eyes with the back of her arm.

Mila let the silence stretch into discomfort.

Brenda suddenly released a deep, sad sigh and met Mila's eyes. "Garrett once shoved a gun in my mouth when he got pissed at me for somethin' stupid. He was high, but still. He knows where I work." She looked away and took a drag off her cigarette with a shaky hand. "I'm sorry."

Disappointment stirred deep in Mila's gut along with a spark of anger. "You should know we found Amelia. She's dead." She stood, grabbed her blazer and stared down at Brenda, watching as her face paled. The woman's gaze flicked to Mila's gun and then back to her eyes. "I guess the question is can you live with yourself if you're helping your abusive ex-boyfriend get away with murdering a child?"

Brenda's head wobbled and she looked nauseated. Still, she clamped her lips together in defiance.

"Come to the Edgewater Police Station and give a new statement. If Garrett Levington is innocent, we can rule him out for good. But if he's not, we can get to the truth now. With your help." She held Brenda's gaze until the woman dropped her head and shook it slightly.

The frustration boiled inside Mila as she started the SUV and flipped the air conditioning on full blast. She pulled up the group text chat that she, Aiden and Frank had going. She typed: *Brenda scared of Levington. Will have to work on her.*

Then she thought about her next move. She really needed to talk to Detective Scott, and he hadn't returned her call yet. She glanced at the time. Almost 6:30 PM. Screw it. She was already in town. Maybe he was still at the station. She pulled up the address for Crystal Harbor PD.

Crystal Harbor PD was a two-story building off a four-lane highway. The lobby was small, just a few cushioned benches, occupied with people filling out paperwork on clipboards There were posters and corkboards on the walls with overlapping flyers and various other notices. She approached the bulletproof window and smiled at the uniformed officer seated behind it. Holding up her badge, she said, "Detective Harlow from Edgewater PD. I'd like to speak with Detective Scott if he's in?"

Sharp eyes gave her the quick, assessing glance that's ingrained in every cop and then a brief nod. "Let me check for you." He picked up the phone and spoke into it. When he hung up, he said, "Yeah, he's here. He'll be right out."

"Thank you." Mila moved away from the desk and walked over to the opposite wall from the door that led to the inner workings of the department. She wanted to watch him before he saw her. Detective Scott's demeanor would tell her a lot about how she should approach him. This could be a minefield. No detective wants to be reminded they failed to find a missing child. Especially not a child who's now turned up dead.

She didn't have to wait long. Detective Scott pushed through the door and glanced around. He spotted her immediately.

She didn't move. Instead, she watched him as he traveled quickly across the lobby with long, purposeful strides. He was tall with shoulders slightly curved inward, wearing black slacks and a dark blue dress shirt, sleeves rolled up and the top button undone. Wavy, chestnut-brown hair brushed his shoulders and gave him a boyish, disheveled look. But when he reached her, and their eyes met, his were dark, sharp and intelligent. She also caught a glimpse of devastation and guilt before he quickly shuttered his emotion. Not quick enough, though.

He obviously wasn't taking this well. She'd have to proceed cautiously if she wanted him as an ally. She held out her hand and as he gave it a brief shake, she said, "Thanks for meeting with me."

"Yeah, sorry I didn't get a chance to return your call." He didn't offer an explanation, but his tone was apologetic. There was a hint of a Southern accent there, too. *Georgia, maybe? Or the Carolinas?* "Come on back. We can talk in the break room."

Mila followed him through the door and down the hallway to the break room with a kitchen set-up and two round tables and chairs. She slid into one of the plastic chairs and watched as he poured two cups of coffee.

"Cream, sugar?" he asked.

"Just cream, thanks." She didn't know if her stomach could take acidic coffee right now, but she wanted to be polite.

He met her gaze and held it as he put the cup down in front of her. Then he lowered himself in the chair across from her. His voice was rough with emotion as he whispered, "So, I heard she was found on Rattlesnake Island."

Mila nodded, still studying him. She was used to being around Aiden, who had a soft, open energy. And Frank, who could be gruff but was always honest. You knew exactly who you were dealing with. She was having a hard time getting a read on this man. He was intense and closed off in a way that made her uncomfortable, but she couldn't put a finger on it.

"Cause of death?" he asked.

"The ME doesn't know yet." She shifted in the hard chair. "What she does know is Amelia was kept alive until about a week ago."

Detective Scott's jaw muscles clenched, his eyes blazed and then darkened. "And I suppose you're wondering what kind of job I did, right? Why in three years couldn't I find her and bring her home before... before she was killed."

And there it is. The defensiveness. Mila didn't take it personally. She knew this was his guilt and frustration talking. Maybe also ego. Still, she didn't appreciate being talked to like that.

"That's a big assumption, Detective Scott."

He glanced up sharply at her, studied her face and then took a purposeful breath. "Sorry. This one just hurts. And it's... personal." He ran a hand over his face, suddenly looking pale and exhausted. "I know they sent over her files. What do you need from me?"

She softened. His pain was real, and it ran deeper than he was letting on. She understood being haunted by not being able to save someone's life.

Her ghosts began with her sister, then her college roommate, Sabine, and then the two domestic violence cases she'd had as a patrol officer. They'd ended with two dead women by their husbands' hands. Not to mention the last case they had worked, the young mother who won't be around to see her little girl grow up. Yeah, she had her own demons. She wouldn't begrudge this man his.

"I need your gut feeling on this. Who was at the top of your list? And has anything changed in the last three years to add to that list?"

He stared at her for an uncomfortably long moment. She let the silence stretch out, let him probe her gaze. Then he suddenly glanced over at the large-faced clock above the microwave. "I'll be glad to share that with you, but I haven't eaten since this morning. Working a burglary case that has me crazy. Care to join me at the Beachside Beat? My treat." His mouth ticked up in a brief, sad smile. "It's the least I can do after snapping at you like that."

Perfect. A more casual setting would help lower his defensive walls.

"I'll follow you."

FIVE

Beachside Beat was a restaurant and waterfront bar owned by a retired Sheriff, and a favorite of local cops. They walked to the outside patio and took a table next to the wooden railing that overlooked the Gulf. The umbrellas above the tables were closed, so the sun was a bit harsh out here. Sunset wasn't for another hour, but the breeze off the water kept things comfortable.

"Hey, Detective." A perky brunette with an eyebrow piercing smiled at Logan as she placed menus in front of them. "Getcha a beer to start? We got the Farmstead IPA in."

"Sounds good, Sarah, thanks."

They both turned to Mila. "Sure, why not? Make that two."

She was technically on duty, but she'd nurse it. Besides, she had to nurture the feeling of camaraderie with Logan Scott, make him let his guard down. If he didn't trust her, feel like she was on his side instead of judging him, he wouldn't share his thoughts about Amelia Larson's case. And the way he had reacted, she didn't trust him. That glint of anger and that ocean of guilt remained beneath the surface. Those strong emotions made for a dangerous combination.

When the waitress left, his eyes narrowed. "I wouldn't have taken you for the IPA type."

"Oh, really?" She leaned her forearms on the table and cocked her head in curiosity. "What type would you have taken me for?"

He also leaned forward, a hint of a smile tugging at the corner of his lips for the first time. His dark gaze held hers for a moment then slowly traveled to the scar down her neck, over to her mouth and took its time meeting her eyes again. His voice was gruff, but his eyes had softened as he said, "Scotch."

His attention on her caused a fluttering in her pulse. Something she hadn't felt for a long time. A gentle laugh escaped her lips. "Scotch?"

"Yes." He leaned back and a wide smile suddenly changed his face, took years off him. "The Scotch drinkers I know are classy and sophisticated, like the complexity of the flavors. They're confident and not intimated by anything bold... in fact, they usually like a challenge."

So, he'd been sizing her up as well. She wasn't sure she agreed with his assessment of her, but she was flattered, nonetheless. Much to her surprise.

They stared at each other as Sarah returned and slid foamy mugs of beer in front of them. "Are we ready to order?"

Logan broke eye contact first and ordered a burger. Mila ordered the crab dip with crackers.

"*Definitely* would've pegged you for a burger guy." Mila smirked after Sarah left. Oh my God, was she flirting? Mila's face warmed and not just from the sun. She lifted the mug of bitter beer to her mouth to hide it.

A deep chuckle came from Logan, and then he lifted his own beer mug. "Cheers, Mila."

Why did the sound of her name in his mouth send a little burst of power through her?

Shaking her head, still mortified with herself, she touched her mug to his. "To uncovering the truth of what happened to Amelia Larson." They both took a deep drink. She cleared her throat. "Speaking of." She raised a brow meaningfully. "Did you ever like the mom's boyfriend for being involved?"

"Cole Richards." Logan sat back in the chair and stared out at the water. In the harsh light, crow's feet were visible at the corners of his coffee-colored eyes. His chest rose and fell in a deep sigh. "He was already in jail when Amelia disappeared. The brother, though. Garrett Levington." His attention swung back to her as his fingers drummed on the side of his mug. "He had a sexual assault on record, and his alibi was his girlfriend. Not very solid."

Mila nodded. "Brenda Creedy? I spoke to her right before I came to see you. She's married to a different guy now, and I think she lied about being with Levington that day, but she's still afraid of him. We'll work on getting her to talk, though." She cocked her head. "Anyone else?"

He hesitated and then nodded. His voice was a growl as he said, "Roman Forester."

"Roman Forester?" She heard the confusion in her own voice. "I know of an Elise Forester, the rich widow who owns a mansion on the bay. She donates frequently to Edgewater charities."

"Yep. Roman is her son. He's an artist and spent most of his life traveling, but he came to Edgewater six months before Amelia Larson disappeared to live with his mother. She apparently has dementia, so he came home to take care of her." He leaned forward, resting his forearms on the table as he clutched his mug. "He's kind of an enigma. Was on Forbes Most Influential Creators list in 2015. Keeps to himself but is active with his money. Local charities and politician fundraisers like his mother. He's become pretty powerful behind the scenes but keeps a low profile."

Mila took all that in. "And what's his connection with Amelia?"

His dark brows lifted. "She was the first child he painted when he moved here."

A spark of recognition made Mila sit up straighter. "Oh, Bobby Sue has a painting of Amelia, some kind of fantasy portrait."

Logan shifted in his seat, nodding. "That would be his."

"Huh. Definitely talented." Mila watched a pair of gray pelicans glide across the surface of the water. Their eight-foot wingspan and large, pouched beaks made them look more like elegant dinosaurs than birds. After they splashed into the water in tandem for a meal, she met his eyes again. "How would Bobby Sue afford a painting from an influential artist like that?"

He swallowed a mouthful of beer and shot her a meaningful look. "That's the thing. He didn't charge her."

She sat up straighter. "Really? Did he know her?"

"Nope. Bobby Sue said he saw Amelia at the beach and just asked if he could paint her."

The hair rose on Mila's arms. This felt significant. "He was stalking little girls at the beach? That's not creepy at all."

Sarah was back. She placed their food in front of them. The scent of hot grease and seafood mingled with the salty breeze. "Getcha anything else?"

"All good for now, thanks," Logan said, distracted. He grabbed the ketchup bottle and squeezed it onto his fries. "His mother said he was at the house painting at the time of the abduction. A nurse confirmed seeing him there. But..."

Mila tore open a cracker package. "But a mother will protect her child at all costs, and that kind of money can buy alibis." She spread the crab dip on a cracker. "Did you have anything else?"

Logan took a bite and then wiped his mouth with a napkin. He shook his head. "Nothing."

She tried to read him, but his eyes remained cast down. "Did you interview him?"

"I asked. He declined."

"Wow. Okay."

They ate in silence for a few moments, both lost in thought. The thrum of voices around them grew louder as the tables began to fill up with a late dinner crowd.

Mila turned toward the restaurant door and froze.

Paul walked in with a grin plastered on his face and Max panting at his side. On his arm was Elly Prescott, the reporter. She also had a grin on her face as they talked. In fact, she was all white teeth, glistening blond hair, long, tan legs in a power skirt and confidence.

Mila felt a rush of heat in her face that burned a trail down to her gut. She was aware that Logan was watching her carefully, but she couldn't stop her reaction.

Elly Prescott? Is that who Paul is seeing? Is that whose toothbrush she saw in his bathroom? She swallowed hard but still couldn't get herself unfrozen.

She could only watch helplessly as they headed to the bar and took up two stools on the end, facing her. The bartender, Graves, came around with a bowl of water for Max, and the dog lapped at it greedily. Graves clapped Paul on the shoulder and said something that had them both shaking their heads.

It used to be her and Paul sitting there sharing stories with Graves. Now he was smiling at Elly, running a hand through his hair like he was fucking charmed.

With every fiber of her being, Mila wanted to flee. She was about to mumble something about the restroom when Max lifted his head from the bowl, his nose sniffing the air. Suddenly he was staring straight at her, ears forward, strings of watery drool hanging from his jaw.

No. No. No, Max.

His tail swished back and forth, and he let out a low woof.

Mila squeezed her eyes shut. This could not be happening.

"Friend of yours?" Logan asked.

She opened her eyes. Logan's head was turned, looking behind him at Max.

But Paul was also staring down at his dog. Then over toward their table. She saw the moment Paul saw her. His eyes flicked to Logan, and he went still. He said something to Elly and then slid off the stool.

"Mila? You okay?" Logan asked under his breath. He reached out his hand and rested it beside hers on the table like he was offering her a lifeline.

She nodded, but she was numb. Her brain was going over all the implications of Paul with Elly. Was Paul the leak in the department? "My ex," she managed.

Paul was suddenly standing at their table. His hard gaze flicked from Detective Scott to Mila. Paul was still in uniform from the waist down: khaki pants, duty belt, and black boots but had changed into a plain black T-shirt that stretched tight across his muscular chest and arms.

Mila focused her attention on Max as Paul said, "Didn't expect to see you here. Any updates on the Amelia Larson case?"

She looked up at him abruptly. *Was he kidding?* He was canoodling with the reporter who would give her left arm for that information. Glancing meaningfully in Elly's direction, her eyes narrowed. "Not yet." She reached over and scratched Max behind the ears, giving herself precious time to recover.

Max rested a paw on her leg, his intelligent eyes holding hers. He could feel her distress.

She forced her shoulders to relax, forced a breath into her lungs. "This is Detective Logan Scott. Crystal Harbor PD." Okay, her voice was surprisingly steady. She could do this. "He was the lead on Amelia's disappearance."

Paul reached forward and shook Logan's offered hand, holding it longer than necessary. Mila felt his energy darken.

Paul had always been protective of her, if not a little possessive. He let her do whatever she wanted, but any man around her did not get that same privilege. She was more than surprised to see him still acting that way. Especially considering his present hot date.

Logan's mouth hinted at a smile as he sat back. Of course, one alpha male recognized the unspoken threat from another alpha male. The silent language was in their DNA. "Beautiful dog you got there," Logan said in an obvious effort to relieve some of the tension. "Search and rescue?"

"Narcotics." Paul was eyeing Logan, his jaw muscles jumping. His smile didn't reach his eyes.

Mila kept her hand on Max, digging into his fur. It was comforting as she watched Paul. He wasn't happy about something. Maybe she's mistaking his signals. Maybe his anger isn't about her but about Detective Scott? Is he judging him for not finding Amelia?

She glanced over at Elly.

Elly had a glass of white wine in one hand, with the other she waved her fingertips and showed off her camera-ready smile.

Mila let her lips curve up in an answering smile, but behind them, her teeth clenched until her jaw ached.

Paul focused his attention back on Mila. "I was going to call you anyway. I know you're going to be neck-deep in this case so I can take Harper to her Krav Maga class tomorrow night."

She searched his face for an answer to his dark mood. It was closed to her. "Your mom was going to take her, but sure if you have the time. She'd love that."

"Okay, then. I'll leave you two to your... dinner." He turned to Logan. "Nice to meet you, Detective."

Logan gave a nod and a tight smile.

Paul let his eyes meet Mila's one last time, a flash of warning in them and then said, "Come on, Max."

Mila watched him take his seat once again next to Elly as Max settled under his feet. Watched her place her hand on his knee. Her stomach filled with acid. "Well, at least Prescott has the decency not to come over and question me about the case here," she said.

"She's a real piece of work. Caught a few minutes of her live broadcast at the dock tonight. Wonder how she got there so fast?" He glanced back at Paul.

"Yeah, I wonder, too."

Logan picked up a fry and popped it in his mouth, still watching her. After he swallowed, he said, "Had a run-in with her last year when she released the name of an armed robbery suspect and tipped him off. Still don't know who gave her that information."

Mila appreciated the fact she wasn't the only one who saw Elly's ambition as dangerous and crossing the line. "Not surprised. She seems to have more than a few willing sources."

"How long has it been?" Logan asked softly. "Since the divorce?"

Mila sighed. "Five years."

Logan raised a brow at that. "And the one daughter?"

She nodded, and pushed her plate away, no longer hungry. "What about you? Married? Kids?" She needed to take the focus off herself. And she needed a drink. She took a long pull from the chilled beer mug and licked at the foam on her top lip.

"Nah. Never been. And no kids." Pain flashed in his eyes with the kind of intensity that would burn a person to the ground if it was ever let out of its cage. He quickly glanced away. "It's a cliché I know, but I'm married to the job."

What was that?

Mila watched him curiously. In her experience, the only thing that could cause the kind of pain he was trying to hide was the loss of a loved one. He was telling her more about himself with what he wasn't willing to show her. But that puzzle would have to wait. There was a more important one to be pieced together.

She rubbed the spot between her brows where a headache was starting. She couldn't do this. Not with Paul and Elly sitting twenty feet away. "I'm sorry. Can I take a raincheck for dinner? I really need to…"

He held up his hand. "You don't have to explain. But I will take you up on that raincheck." Pulling a card out of his wallet, he jotted down his cell number and gave it to her. "And I'd appreciate a heads-up with any updates. I got skin in this one, too."

She forced a smile. "I understand."

Mila sat in her SUV in the parking lot. Finally alone, all the emotions rushed up and out of her. Is this how the press got to Rattlesnake Island so quickly? How Elly got there in time for a live broadcast? How she found out it was a young girl? Did Paul call Elly after she left the house?

She squeezed the steering wheel, the anger, the frustration, the sense of betrayal, flowing like lava burning through her veins, coming out in hot tears rolling down her cheeks. She let them fall. After a few minutes the fatigue set in. Her shoulders slumped.

He wouldn't do that, would he? Not the Paul she knew. But who knows what kind of spell a beautiful woman like Elly can weave?

Well, actually Mila did.

She suddenly felt like she was back in high school, where she'd had a crush on the boys' swim team captain, Olin Knight, and he seemed to feel the same until Britney Jacobs, senior cheerleader, took an interest in him, too. Their cute banter and flirting stopped, and Olin was completely under Britney's spell.

A buzz alerted her to an incoming text. It was from Paul: *You really think dating another cop is going to go any better the second time?*

Mila sat stunned, staring at her phone. *Is he kidding? Is he really trying to dictate who she dates while he cuddles up to a reporter?* "Not that it's any of your business, but it wasn't a date," she barked, throwing her phone into the passenger seat.

Ignoring him and the scathing reply she wanted to fire off, she moved her attention to the beauty of the setting sun in all its fluorescent orange glory, took a few deep breaths, and reminded herself there was no time to waste on her feelings or personal life. She had a job to do.

She pulled up the group text and typed: *Still at the station?*

Aiden: *We're all here.*

Be there in fifteen.

Six

Mila found them in the conference room, next to Captain Bartol's office. They all wore frustrated expressions with ties and jackets removed and flung over chairs. Open pizza boxes filled the room with the scent of grease and tomato sauce. She took the empty chair next to Aiden.

"Hungry?" Aiden asked, pushing one of the boxes toward her.

"Thanks, but just had a bite with Detective Scott to see if he had any new insights or suspects." She had barely eaten, but her stomach would reject food right now.

"How'd that go?" Frank asked. He was sticking a plastic spoon in a microwave bowl of oatmeal. He held up a hand. "Actually, Captain's going to be here in a few. She's just finishing up a call with Mayor Starek. Might want to wait so you don't have to repeat yourself."

Mila nodded as she cracked open a bottled water, swallowed two Tylenol she'd grabbed from her desk and glanced up at the murder board where they did their thinking out loud.

Amelia Larson's school photo was tacked to the top. Cole Richards and Garrett Levington's names were beneath with some pertinent dates and other information.

Mila stood, grabbed the marker and wrote Roman Forester's name beside theirs.

"New suspect? Did Detective Scott give you that?" Aiden asked around a mouthful of cheese pizza.

Mila shrugged. "Someone to look into." She glanced over at Matt. He was in his wheelchair, reading something intently with one hand, a piece of half-eaten pizza in the other. "Want to share with the class?" she asked teasingly.

He glanced up, dark eyes shining under jet-black spiked bangs and grinned. "Just some new technology I'll be trying to get us to help crack cell phones quicker."

Mila returned a genuine smile.

Matt Lee was a detective in his early forties. He had been in a bad car accident five years ago that had severed his spinal cord, which left him in a wheelchair. He could no longer work in the field, but he hadn't wanted to retire either. Captain Bartol worked hard to get grants to buy a forensic computer and send him to get certified in digital forensics. He was a natural.

The captain strode in, distraction pinching her brows together. She glanced around the table and then took a seat next to Frank. "All right, what do we have?"

Frank spoke first. "I found Cole Richards through his parole officer. He's got a new job cleaning boats, but same shitty attitude. Told me to go fuck myself when I asked if he'd seen his brother since he's been out. Still blames Bobby Sue Larson for his three-year stint."

"She said he's been calling her. We need to warn him off harassing her," Mila said.

"I'll gladly take care of that," Frank said.

"What about the brother in Odessa? Garrett Levington?" Captain Bartol asked.

Aiden wiped at his mouth with a napkin and held up a finger. "Didn't get much from him, but took a look around his property. He's got places he could've hid the girl."

Her eyes narrowed in thought. "But he had an alibi?"

Mila spoke up. "Yes, but I spoke to his alibi today, ex-girlfriend Brenda Gorski. She's currently married to a different guy. I got the feeling she lied for Levington, but she's too scared to come clean."

Captain Bartol sighed. "I don't know if her changing her story will be useful to us anyway. Defense cross-examination will destroy her as a witness since she lied to us before. Easy to make it out as revenge if she frees him up now." She tapped her fingers on the table. "All right. Let's bring her into the station anyway, put some pressure on her. If Garrett Levington's alibi falls apart, and he won't come clean about where he was, we'll try to get a search warrant for that property." She glanced up at the board. "Roman Forester? Isn't he that famous painter?"

"Yep." Mila folded her hands on the table, noticed the sparkly pink polish she'd let Harper paint them for her sister's celebration of life, and then shoved them back under the table. Clearing her throat, she said, "I had a conversation with Detective Logan Scott. He said Forester moved to Edgewater a few months before Amelia was abducted to take care of his mother with dementia. He saw Amelia on the beach one day, asked her mother if he could paint her. Detective Scott couldn't get him in for an interview, and he didn't have any evidence to take it further. Just a gut feeling I guess."

Captain Bartol glanced from her to the board. "Interesting. Okay, worth looking into."

"Do you know anything about Detective Scott?" Mila asked.

The captain turned her attention back to Mila. "I've heard good things about him. Thorough with the job. You get a different vibe?"

"No, just want to know what I'm dealing with. He seems steeped in guilt about this case." *Or something more personal.*

Her shoulders lifted. "That's understandable."

"One thing that's really bothering me," Mila said, changing the subject. "Why the birthday crown? It wasn't her birthday. And obviously it meant something to her or the killer, otherwise when he or she dumped the body, they wouldn't have bothered to bring the crown."

"That is odd," Aiden agreed.

"She was wearing a fancy dress, too," Frank said. "Like she'd been at a party."

"Obviously it was a one-child party," Matt said.

"And you checked the database for similar MOs?" Captain asked.

"Yep. But I'll check again when we have more information."

Captain Bartol pursed her lips. "Okay, so we bring in Brenda Gorski tomorrow and look into Roman Forester more thoroughly. What else have we got?"

Mila checked her notes. "When Amelia disappeared from the festival, Bobby Sue was talking to her friend Shelby Myers. We need to get a new statement from her. See if time has changed her story or helped her remember anything."

"I'll find her tomorrow," Aiden volunteered.

Mila nodded. "I'll go talk to Forester in the morning. Also, I'm going to spend a few more hours going through the files tonight."

"I'll help," Aiden said.

"I can stay, too," Frank added.

Captain Bartol gave Frank a look. "You go home, get some rest. In the morning, you can pick up Brenda Gorski."

He looked like he was going to argue but then his shoulders fell. He began gathering up his notebook and empty oatmeal cup.

"You guys find anything for me to dig into, let me know," Matt said.

Mila went to her desk and video-called Kittie.

As soon as Kittie answered, she blurted out, "Did you know Paul is dating Elly Prescott?" She'd tried to keep her tone non-accusatory but failed. She realized at that moment she felt a tinge of betrayal with Kittie too, which was dumb. Paul was her son, of course she'd be loyal to him.

Kittie's watery blue eyes softened, and she sighed. "Yes. You know I try to stay out of you kids' business but honestly, I'm not sure what he's thinking. That gal seems like she'd do anything for a story." She rested her chin on a small fist. "And just so you know, I haven't met her."

Mila slumped in the chair. "I saw them tonight. At a restaurant. I hope to God he's not feeding her information."

"Oh, hon. He wouldn't do that."

"Well, she's getting it from somewhere." Mila rubbed her forehead. "Anyway, sorry, didn't mean to put you in a tough spot. Is Harper around?"

"Don't you dare apologize. You know you're like a daughter to me. She's upstairs, hang on." She called for Harper.

While they waited, Kittie asked how the case was going.

"We've got a few suspects," Mila said, trying to stay positive.

Harper's face appeared. Her bearded dragon, Iggy, sat on her shoulder. She launched right into the conversation with her usual enthusiasm. "Guess what?"

"What?"

"We had a monkey bars race at recess today, and I beat Mason!"

"I'm sure he loved that." Mila felt the tension in her chest unfurl as she watched the sparkle in her daughter's eyes, the mischief in her dimpled smile.

"He said I cheated." She rolled her eyes and Mila caught a glimpse of the teen years heading her way too quickly. "Like you can cheat on monkey bars. Are you coming home soon?

Grandma Kittie made chicken pot pies. I helped and made my own."

"I have to stay late tonight. We have a big case." She hesitated. Harper had been so upset three years ago when she'd heard about Amelia's disappearance. She didn't want her to know they'd found the girl dead. But she also knew her daughter would hear about it eventually at school so better to hear about it from her, right? "Remember the girl who went missing a few years ago? Amelia Larson?"

"Yeah," Harper's eyes lit up. "Did you find her?"

"Yes, honey, but it's not in the way we would have liked."

"Oh." Her gaze fell. Her small hand went to Iggy's back for comfort. "She's dead."

"We're going to do everything we can to catch the person who did it, make sure they don't hurt anyone else. That's why I can't come home. Do you understand?" If Mila had known it would be this hard to be a cop with a kid, she'd have become an accountant or some other desk job.

"Yes. You and Dad catch the bad guys," she said with a deep sigh.

Mila's heart squeezed. Of course a ten-year-old just wants their parents' attention. They don't care how noble a cause it is that steals them away. "That's right. Speaking of Dad, he's going to be able to take you to your Krav Maga class tomorrow night."

Harper pursed her lips in thought, a touch of sadness still swimming in her blue eyes. "Okay. Do you think he can take me to get Iggy some crickets after?"

"I'm sure he will." Mila forced a smile. "Better him than me."

Mila got off the phone, her smile fading, wondering if she did the right thing by telling Harper about Amelia Larson's fate.

"Something you want to talk about?" Aiden had turned in his chair, a pile of folders on his lap.

Mila clutched her necklace, sliding the half-moon back and forth on the silver chain for comfort. "I told Harper we found Amelia. Didn't want her to hear it from kids in school. Not sure I should've without being there to talk if she needs it, though."

"Kittie's there," he said.

Mila's distress deepened and it must've shown on her face.

"Hey, stop it. No guilt. You can't be in two places at once, and you're doing the best you can." A gruff laugh escaped him. "At least that's what I tell myself when Meredith calls overwhelmed with the girls."

"Three girls under six." Mila shook her head. "You better get her diamonds for Christmas."

"For that, I'd have to get a different job. Which would actually be a much better Christmas present."

They shared a laugh, then got back to work.

After working in companionable silence for a while, Aiden said, "There were no cameras at the Seafood Festival, but they asked the public to turn in any photos or video around that time. There's a flash drive here, I'll give it to Matt in the morning."

Mila nodded. "I'm not seeing anywhere Detective Scott let anything fall through the cracks. All known sex offenders in the area were interviewed and accounted for. Seems his main suspect was Garrett Levington."

"Makes sense since most of the time, it is family or a family friend."

She read the file. "But he pulled the black box from Levington's F-150 and sent it to a company to be analyzed. When he got it back, it showed the truck in Odessa, driving to a park. Didn't move until six that night. Brenda said they were fishing in the lake there all day."

"He could've parked it for an alibi, knowing that would be checked."

"I don't think he's that smart." She flipped through the papers and came to a printout of Garrett's phone logs. She scanned them. "This is interesting. He did get a call from his brother from prison the day before Amelia disappeared. Someone highlighted it."

Aiden scooted his chair forward and began to empty out the last box. "Let's see if there's a copy of that conversation here."

It took them about ten minutes to find the evidence bag with the thumb drive labeled with the two-party conversation between the brothers and the date. Mila stuck it in her computer as Aiden maneuvered his chair beside hers.

It was a quick conversation. A few seconds of warm-up—how's everything, did you get my stuff into your storage shed, etc. Then the last request made them sit up. It was Cole. "I need you to pick up that Christmas ham. You know what to do with it."

"Goddamnit, Cole. I don't want to be involved in your shit. I got enough heat on me."

"You owe me."

"Fine. Don't drop the soap in there, little bro." Garrett hung up, obviously angry.

"Christmas ham?" Aiden's brows were pushed up into his hairline.

Mila's breathing increased with a jolt of excitement. "Let's find Garrett Levington's interrogation. They had to ask him about that."

"I saw the taped interviews in box number two." Aiden wheeled around the desk, a new urgency in his motions.

They found the interview labeled *Garrett Levington* with the date of the interview and went back to Mila's computer. She clicked the keys and brought up the image of the interview room at Crystal Harbor PD.

"Shit," she said, when she saw a man in a cheap suit sitting next to Levington and across from Detective Scott. She turned up the volume but knew what they were going to hear.

"He lawyered up." Aiden sounded as dejected as she felt.

The lawyer wasn't letting him answer any questions. When Detective Scott asked about the "Christmas ham" comment, Levington's slow smile and silence made Mila want to punch the monitor. She couldn't imagine the frustration Detective Scott was feeling at that moment. Well, actually she could, and her heart went out to him.

The lawyer motioned for Garrett to get up as he stated, "We're done here."

Detective Scott didn't watch them leave. He closed his notebook, folded his hands into fists and leaned his forehead on them.

Mila clicked off the video, feeling like she was invading his privacy.

"If Brenda Gorski comes clean, we can use that to have another conversation with Levington at least. Maybe after all this time, he'll feel confident enough that we don't have anything to come in without a lawyer."

"That's a big maybe. Worth a shot though. Let's hope Frank can get somewhere with Brenda tomorrow."

By the time they finished going through the boxes and jotting down any questions, or anything to follow up on, it was almost midnight.

Frank returned with a plastic container of salad and more color in his face. He glanced at the two of them. "Give me whatever needs following up tonight. You two look like shit. Go home and grab a few hours of sleep."

Mila was going to argue, but she was having a hard time getting her brain to process simple sentences. "Deal." She gathered up her notes and handed them to Frank. "See you in a few hours but call if there are any breaks."

Aiden pushed himself out of the chair and stretched his back. "Your turn to bring the good coffee in the morning."

—※—

Mila was running through a dark forest, tree branches scraping her arms. Her eyes flew open, and she stared into a set of deep brown ones. Oscar let out a sharp *woof* as he pawed her arm one more time. Mila flung the covers off and jumped up, following him back to Harper's bedroom.

Harper's soft whimpers filled the room.

"Sh sh sh, sweetie." Mila scooped Harper up in her arms. Her daughter's face was wet with tears, her body damp with sweat. She was all lanky arms and legs. When had she gotten so tall? She opened her eyes, and her sobs began to calm down as she became aware of her mom.

"I had a bad dream," she hiccupped.

"I know. I'm here. It wasn't real." She snuggled Harper's head under her chin, rocking her. "You're completely safe."

"It was so scary though. A man was chasing me down the beach, and I knew he took Amelia, and he was going to kill me next."

This was Mila's fault. She shouldn't have told her about Amelia's fate. Mila felt tears prickling her eyes. "I'm sorry that was such a scary dream. But you know Dad and I would never let anything happen to you."

Harper pulled away and looked into her mom's eyes. Glass blue eyes, the same color as Paul's but softer, still full of innocence. "What if you're not here?"

Mila helped her lay back down and then scooted in beside her, pulling the covers over both of them. *Yeah, that was a great question. Even if I wanted to be, I couldn't always be there to protect my daughter.* "Kittie would never let anything happen to you, either. Or Oscar."

At the sound of his name, Oscar hopped on the bed, turned a few circles and then laid across their feet. His weight was an immediate comfort. "See? He knows his job is to protect you. Go back to sleep. I'll stay here."

Mila stared at the ceiling until Harper's soft snores started. An image of Amelia decomposing in the morgue drawer came unbidden. She pulled Harper's body into her own and closed her eyes. If only she could freeze this moment. This moment her daughter was safe in her arms. If only every child could always be safe, no matter where they were. That is what she'd give her right arm for... no, not just her right arm... her life.

SEVEN

Mila managed to get two hours of sleep before her restless mind had her slipping quietly out of Harper's bed and into a hot shower. She'd dressed but was still groggy as she returned to Harper's room to kiss her goodbye and stepped in a pile of dog vomit.

"Shit," she hissed. Hopping back out, she removed her shoe and threw it in the tub to wash before tiptoeing downstairs to retrieve carpet cleaner and paper towels.

After she cleaned up the mess as best she could, she silently made her way to where Oscar was lying in the corner of the room. Kneeling, she stroked his head and assessed him. He threw up once in a while like all dogs, but he seemed more lethargic this morning. Also, he wasn't stretched across Harper's bed.

A big red flag.

She gave him a scratch under the ear, noting he didn't wag his tail. Another red flag.

After tossing the mess in the outside garbage can, and sliding into her SUV, she texted Kittie: *Oscar threw up in Harper's room. Please make a vet appt. today. Thnx.*

With that done, she was on the road by six AM, headed to The Pour House, her mother's coffee shop.

The Pour House was located on Mango Avenue in the Historic Commons in the heart of downtown Edgewater. The Commons was a five-block grid of restaurants, breweries, whimsical shops, a local museum, and the Farmer's Market, with brick sidewalks and bronze antique lantern-style light poles. In the center of the grid sat Manatee Park, a small grassy area for picnicking around the fountain. A large bronze sea turtle statue painted in tropical colors by a local artist graced the entrance to the park. Pinellas bike trail, a forty-five-mile paved trail, ran right through the middle of it and brought in traffic to the restaurants and shops.

The small coffee shop had pine floors, reclaimed from a torn-down beach mansion, floor-to-ceiling bookshelves and a large chandelier sparkling above the array of cozy tables. The early morning crowd was usually working professionals and early gym-goers who appreciated the healthier protein muffins on offer.

But today she stood in line behind a young father, his baby girl snuggled in a carrier strapped to the front of his body. He bounced a little on his toes whenever the baby got fussy and rubbed her head. Mila watched him order two lattes to go. He must be giving his wife time to take a shower.

Mila remembered those days. The days of sleep deprivation, constant anxiety over keeping a brand new human alive, emotional turmoil and so much love it hurt. It felt like yesterday. Paul being a daily part of her life felt like yesterday.

"Good morning, my darling girl." Behind the counter, Mila's mom looked her over with an assessing gaze and frowned. "Need an extra shot? You don't look like you slept."

"I tried, but I'd told Harper about Amelia, and she had a nightmare. Better give an extra shot to everybody. There will be no sleeping tonight, either. I need five coffees and a box of blueberry protein muffins."

"Got it and hey," she gave Mila a knowing nod, "better she find out from you." She released her gaze and grabbed a box and tongs. She kept her voice low when she asked, "You guys have any leads on the monster who took little Amelia yet?"

Mila was still feeling grateful for her mom's comment, reaffirming it was better that Harper heard the bad news from her. It made her feel a little better. She shrugged. "A few things to follow up on."

"I'm going to have Kittie and Harper over for dinner this week. I know she'll be missing you."

"They'd love that. I know they've missed you, too."

As Mila pushed open the coffee shop door, she happened to look up and notice a man in a black hoodie standing against the wall across the street. His arms were crossed, and he seemed to be staring straight at her, but she couldn't see his face. An alarm went off in her nervous system. He could be waiting for someone inside, but it was the way he was poised, still and ready to strike like a predator, that had her suddenly breathing hard. Plus, the morning was already too warm for a hoodie.

She glanced down the sidewalk and spotted Roadie. He was a thirty-something homeless man who had been hit by a drunk driver twelve years ago and gotten addicted to pain meds, which led to a heroin addiction. After he'd been busted in a drug sting two years ago, she'd tried to get him into a program to get him off the streets and in a rehab program but had failed. So, for now, she did what she could to keep him alive.

Moving briskly down the sidewalk toward him, she dug a muffin out of the bag. "Morning, Roadie."

"Mornin', Detective."

She handed him the muffin and a coffee from the tray, then motioned behind her. "Hey, have you noticed that guy in the hoodie standing there for long?"

He lifted his head and peered across the street from beneath a worn baseball cap. "What guy?"

She jerked her gaze back across the street. The guy was gone.

"Never mind." She forced a smile. Maybe she was just being paranoid.

—✳—

Mila carried the tray of coffee and bag of muffins to her desk. Frank and Aiden filed in a few minutes later. Mila realized too late she shouldn't have got Frank a coffee.

He did grab a muffin though as Aiden began to fill him in on what they found out last night.

At seven AM Captain Bartol arrived with Matt rolling in right behind her.

"Thanks for the coffee, Mila," the captain said, as she plucked a Pour House cup from the tray. "You two get anything from the files last night?"

"Yep." Aiden dug out the flash drive from his bag and handed it to Matt. "This is all the video footage and photos from the festival Crystal Harbor PD collected from the public. See if you can find anything they missed."

Mila sipped her coffee, then said, "There was also a suspicious call Cole made to his brother from prison the night before Amelia disappeared. Levington lawyered up and wouldn't answer for it, but we're hoping to get him in again, now that time has passed."

Aiden turned to Frank. "If you can get anywhere with Brenda today, I'll bring him in."

Frank had his hands shoved in the pockets of his black slacks. "I'm not worried. She'll talk."

Mila eyed him, having no doubt. Frank was good at finding people's weaknesses and going for the metaphorical throat.

"All right, team." The captain shot them a serious look. "I don't have to tell you how time-sensitive this is. Let's push hard today. I've been holding off on a press conference, but Sheila wants one soon with something to give them."

Sheila Starek has been mayor of Edgewater for twelve years now, re-elected because of her tireless work to keep the town affordable for residents without compromising their small beach town roots.

When everyone got to work, Mila checked her emails while she ate her protein muffin and finished her coffee. At eight-thirty, she headed out to have a chat with Mr. Forester.

The morning was overcast. A dark layer of clouds blocked the sun and floated eastward. It matched her mood perfectly as she pulled up to the iron gates on Harbor Drive. She rolled down her window and punched the call box on the gate.

"Yes? Can I help you?" a female voice crackled over the speaker.

"Detective Mila Harlow, Edgewater PD. I need to speak to Roman Forester."

A few moments of silence followed then the gates rumbled to life and rolled open. Mila pulled into a courtyard with established, lush landscaping and a fountain in the center of a circle driveway. She parked in front of the two-story Spanish Colonial-style mansion with a creamy white stucco exterior and a red barrel tile roof. The mother had been living there as a widow since her surgeon husband passed twenty years ago. Mila had no idea about her and Roman's relationship. Were they close? Did Roman visit his mother often before he moved in? He must care about her if he's willing to move in now that she has dementia. This at least speaks to his character.

After climbing the wide semi-circle of steps, she knocked on the thick wooden doors.

A gray-haired woman in a crisp black and white maid uniform opened them. "Come in, Detective."

Mila stepped into the cavernous entrance with shiny white marble beneath her feet, floor-to-ceiling arched windows to her right, and a wall of sliding glass doors to the left. A whiff of lemon polish hung in the air. Large crystal chandeliers scattered their light across the floor. The furniture looked like something from medieval England with ornate, heavy cherry wood and tufted leather sofas. Her attention moved to the curved stairway in the middle, framed by two thick Roman pillars. Her gaze followed the stairs upward. Definitely enough rooms up there to hide a little girl away from the world.

"This way, ma'am." The maid led her past the wall of glass doors, where she caught a glimpse of a pool, a sky-blue rectangle nestled in a dark green lawn. The expanse of Bay waters loomed beyond the edge of the lawn.

They passed the stairs and turned right. Mila paused and stared at the giant painting of a nude Marilyn Monroe centered on the wall. The actress was perched on a white bed, staring at the viewer head-on, wearing nothing but a gold and red Queen's crown and her classic soft smile. It was actually beautiful and tastefully done, the soft strokes making her look like a mirage or a dream. Forester's signature was in the bottom right corner.

The maid waited for her to finish admiring the painting and then continued leading her into a living room where a fire was burning in a massive stone fireplace. A woman in a wheelchair sat in front of it, a blanket across her lap.

"Have a seat. Mr. Forester will be right with you."

When she left, Mila walked over to the woman. Her face was blank, her gaze locked on the fire. She cleared her throat. "Hello. Mrs. Forester?"

The woman blinked and looked up. Her gray hair was curled and sprayed in place. Though wrinkles were deep around her brown eyes, her skin was powdered and blushed. A diamond bracelet caught the light as her hand fluttered to her neck. In her other arm, she cradled a baby doll, a girl with blonde ringlets in a lacey, pink dress. "Who are you?"

Mila had never met anyone with dementia before. She wasn't sure what to expect. "I'm Detective Mila Harlow. I'm here to speak to your son. I just wanted you to know I'm in the room, so I didn't startle you."

Her face morphed from confusion to anger then sadness. She stroked the doll's shiny hair with a veiny hand. "Ramona's a good girl. Just misunderstood."

Did she think the doll was a real baby? Seems like she chose a name close to her son's, so maybe. Mila didn't know what to say. She didn't want to upset the woman, so she just kept quiet.

Luckily Roman arrived at that moment. "Ah, Detective."

She watched him approach. He was a tall man, early fifties with curly salt and pepper hair and a heavy layer of jewelry around his neck and wrists. Despite a prominent limp, he moved across the room with the confidence of a man used to getting what he wanted. "Sorry to keep you waiting. I was just working on a new painting." He reached her and held out a hand.

Mila shook it. His hand was large and soft. The hand of someone who doesn't do manual labor. She glanced at the leg he was favoring. "How'd you hurt your leg?"

He waved off her question. "Oh, I have a pin in it, an old injury. So, what can I do for you today?"

Guess they were getting right down to business. "I'm sure you've heard we found Amelia Larson?" She watched his face carefully. Something sparked in his eyes. Recognition or something more sinister?

He glanced over at his mother in the wheelchair, who had returned to quietly staring into the fire, then motioned for Mila to follow him.

He led her through the sliding glass doors, and they took a seat poolside beneath a large white canvas umbrella. A break in the clouds left a patch of sparkling sun on the face of the water.

She moved her gaze from the stunning view to the man as he spoke. "I did hear about Amelia's remains being found—devastating news. She was a sweet girl. I'm not sure how I can help, but whatever you need, I'm at your service."

Mila studied the man. His gray eyes were shuttered, letting no emotion out, and his mouth was set in a thin, neutral line. "I saw the painting you did of Amelia. It's beautiful. Her mother has it hanging in her trailer. Is it true you didn't charge her for it?"

After a quick nod he said, "It was an exchange, not a gift."

Mila's brows rose as a sea breeze lifted her dark hair from where it brushed her shoulders. "Go on."

He shifted in the chair and folded his long, elegant fingers, seemingly searching for the right words to explain. "I immortalized Amelia's spirit for her family, and in return, I got to study and soak up the yet unencumbered essence of the feminine."

Mila stayed silent, careful to keep her own expression neutral, and encouraged him to continue.

His gaze took her in and then he leaned back, lips pursed in thought. "To me, little girls represent the seeds of the feminine aspect of nature. They naturally carry their own worth and truth in their upward-turned chin, and their protruding bellies, because they've not yet learned to suck it in or tone it down. They've not yet been misshaped by the patriarchy to hide their light and power. They are pure potential." He rubbed a bit of red paint off his thumb as he watched her. "I simply want to showcase that power. My way of trying to balance the world we find ourselves in, I suppose."

Mila's thoughts drifted to Harper. She knew he was right. That one day, she would be teased about her body and shamed. She would inevitably learn the lessons all little girls learn when puberty strikes and they must shrink themselves, become small and quiet to stay safe from unwanted attention.

She pulled herself away from those thoughts. She needed to understand his mindset. He seemed to be obsessed with little girls, which didn't bode well for him, despite being a good son. "What do you mean by balance the world?"

He cocked his head, and a small, fleeting smile graced his lips. "Balance the power dynamics. As they grow up, children slowly learn that the feminine is excluded from holding power in every aspect of the world we've built... religion, politics, family hierarchies. It is changing, but very slowly and not without setbacks. Through my art I try to contribute to raising the feminine, giving it equal respect, attention and energy. That's what I mean by balance."

She was starting to understand. Whether she believed it was the truth or he was feeding her a line of bullshit, she wasn't sure. "So, what I'm hearing is your interest in young girls is simply to help empower women?"

He let his eyes roam over her scar and down to her gun. Then he nodded. "Empowered women in this world are still shaped by the blade. By pain. By aligning with the masculine's idea of power. They set their gaze outward on the world instead of inward, where their true power lies." He reached up and adjusted the layer of necklaces at his throat, thick water pearl, along with various gold styles and lengths. "People are in pain, Mother Earth is in pain... and yet, the inner wisdom of the feminine, the thing that can heal these wounds, is ridiculed as weak and murdered in childhood." A sad chuckle escaped his lips. "Maybe that should be your next case, Detective."

She offered him a brief smile. He was interesting, she'd give him that. Somewhere in his little speech was a spark that resonated within her, something that touched both shame and fury.

She cleared her throat and moved her attention across the Bay waters to the bit of land that was Rattlesnake Island. "I'm sure you heard Amelia was found there." She lifted her chin toward the island and made eye contact.

He nodded his head slightly but didn't answer.

She turned to stare at the forty-foot Bayliner yacht tucked into his private dock. "When was the last time you took your yacht for a spin?"

His mouth twitched in amusement. "It's been at least three months." He leaned forward. "Let's cut to the chase, Detective. I had nothing to do with Amelia Larson's abduction or death. I would never harm a child. I hold them in too much reverence."

She cocked her head. "But you refused to give an interview to Detective Logan Scott when Amelia first disappeared. Why?"

His top lip curled up in distaste. "I found him to be judgmental, and I don't waste my time or energy with judgmental people."

She raised a brow skeptically and waited for more.

His body shifted and jerked in irritation. "His eyes were full of contempt. For my money, for my enjoyment of painting children. I have no idea. Yours... hold no such judgment. Only a search for the truth. I appreciate that." He pushed himself up. "But on that note, I must get back to my painting. You'll see yourself out?"

She stood and handed him a card. "In case you think of anything that could help us. Have a good day, Mr. Forester."

She snapped some photos with her phone of his yacht, and the view of Rattlesnake Island, before she walked back to her SUV. As much as he had opened up to her, it felt like a performance, like he was hiding something big.

⁂

As she walked into the Investigative Division bullpen, she was still rehashing the conversation with Roman Forester. Something was off about him. He was an eccentric artist, yes. But that wasn't it. There was an incongruence. A pattern that didn't fit.

A text came in. It was from Kittie: *Vet thinks Oscar ate something poisonous. Gave him fluids, activated charcoal, keeping him for a few hours for observation. Going to check yard for anything he may have got into.*

Mila stopped in her tracks. They'd made sure there weren't any poisonous plants in the yard. What could he have eaten? She texted back: *thnx. Keep me updated.*

Still concerned, she left her leather satchel by her desk, dropped her Glock in her desk drawer and walked over to join Captain Bartol and Aiden at the monitor where they could watch interviews.

Frank was in the interview room with Brenda Gorski. She had her arms crossed, and her face was a blank mask above the skull tattoo on her neck.

"How long have they been in there?" Mila asked.

"Fifteen minutes or so," Captain Bartol said.

"She came in on her own?" Mila asked.

Aiden shifted on his feet. "Nah. Frank picked her up at her house."

Mila shook her head. "She's tough. And scared. He's going to have to try something other than appealing to her sense of doing the right thing." She had already tried that and failed.

Frank reached down and pulled a folder from his bag.

"I think he just came to the same conclusion," Captain Bartol said.

Mila watched Brenda's face as he opened the folder and slid it in front of her. She didn't have to see it to know it was the autopsy photos of Amelia. She could tell by the sudden horror on Brenda's face, by the way her hands flew up and covered her mouth, and by the way she gagged and turned quickly away.

Frank flipped the folder closed and watched her silently. No remorse.

Her shoulders rose and fell as she sobbed.

He pushed the Kleenex box toward her. A small mercy.

Through hiccups and starts and stops, she finally admitted that Garrett Levington forced her to lie for him. Made her say she was with him all day. She had no idea what he'd really been doing. "But if he did this... he can rot in hell," she cried.

Aiden turned to the captain. "Should I go pick up Garrett Levington?"

She pursed her lips in thought. "No. It's a risk, but I'd rather not tip him off. Write up an affidavit for a search warrant. Don't forget to mention the call from the jail the day before Amelia disappeared and their coded conversation. Judge Matthews might be inclined to sign it, but go see him in person. Let's hope we catch him on a generous day.

EIGHT

They did, in fact, catch him on a generous day. By six that evening they had coordinated with the local Odessa Sheriff's Office and were pulling up onto Garrett Levington's property via a well-worn driveway through pine and scrub brush. Mila, Aiden, one patrol car and one evidence van with two CSI techs followed the local sheriff's car.

As they parked, Garrett Levington burst onto the porch, a beer in his hand, his face blood red.

Mila exited the SUV just in time to hear him shout at the sheriff's deputy. "What the hell is this, J.T.?"

The young deputy held up his hand. "Just calm down, Garrett. These folks from Edgewater PD have a search warrant for your property. I'm sure you got nothin' to hide so just let 'em do their job, and we'll be outa your hair in no time."

Mila stepped up onto the porch and handed Levington the warrant.

He ripped it out of her hand, his eyes narrowing. "Edgewater? This is about Amelia then. I got an alibi for that day."

The deputy lowered his head and then shot Mila a side glance.

Garrett Levington caught it. Rage flashed in his eyes as he understood. "That bitch. You know she's lyin' through her damn teeth to get even with me now."

Aiden moved up the steps to stand beside Mila, hands resting on his hips. "Mr. Levington, we're going to ask you to wait out here while we conduct our search. We're also going to search the shed, so if you don't mind unlocking it."

Aiden had told Mila on the way over that there was a heavy padlock on it.

Garrett's tongue poked in the side of his mouth. He took a sip of his beer and smiled. "And what if I do mind."

"No problem. I have bolt cutters in the car." Aiden turned to go.

"Wait, wait," Garrett cursed as he stomped inside the house and came out with a wad of keys.

"We'll take the shed," Mila said, motioning to P.J. O'Malley and Officer Meyers, the rookie. Then she pointed to the other CSI tech, Rhodes, and Officer Dolan. "You two take the house with Detective Reyes."

Mila didn't miss the resentment radiating off Officer Bobby Dolan. He was a twelve-year veteran of the force, but his request to be moved to the detective division had been denied. No one knew why, because there was an open position since Willy Jackson had retired four months ago. Officer Dolan obviously wasn't taking it well. She tried to stay out of his way.

Mila, Officer Myers and P.J. O'Malley followed Garrett as he walked through the sandy yard to the shed and waited while he unlocked it. Mila noticed a small fishing boat sitting trailered on the side under a blue tarp. That wasn't included in their warrant, so they couldn't touch it.

Too bad.

Garrett glared at them and then shook his head, leaving them alone.

Mila pulled her phone out of her pocket when it buzzed. A new text from Kittie:

Oscar home, resting. Didn't find anything in yard.

Mila was relieved he was home. Hopefully whatever had made him sick wasn't still around. Moving her attention back to the search, she pulled open both doors, and they peered into the dark shadows, the smell of gasoline and damp wood wafting over them. Misshapen objects and some boxes filled the space.

"Doesn't look like any room to keep a kid in here," P.J. noted, securing her long, red hair into a bun and slipping on gloves.

Mila stepped in and ran a gloved hand across the wall, finding a light switch. She flicked it on. "It's been a week, so he could've moved stuff in here to throw us off." She sounded skeptical to own ears, but she was trying to keep an open mind about all the possibilities.

"Okay, Officer Meyers, let's go through every box. We can take anything digital that may be used for recording, laptops, thumb drives, cameras. Also, any children's clothing or other personal items a child may have used. And of course, P.J. you sweep for any hair, fibers or blood."

They went to work with the frogs singing in the pond nearby, the mosquitos buzzing in their ears. There was a light breeze tonight, but it wasn't reaching them inside the wooden structure. Mila's hairline and shirt grew damp as she helped Officer Meyers go through each cardboard box and then they set them outside.

She wasn't sure how much time had passed, sifting through car parts and bottles of various oils and cleaners, when P.J. called from behind a large machine. "I got possible blood drops."

Mila carefully picked her way through a narrow path in the mess and crouched down beside P.J., who was snapping photos of the spots. She pointed a gloved finger at two brown stains on the floor about the size of dimes. Mila nodded. "Test it."

P.J. pulled her backpack off and got out her own tools. Uncapping a thin tube of distilled water, she squeezed a few drops on a cotton swab. She swabbed the edge of one of the brown spots. Then she pulled out a plastic tube of Quick Check, crushed the two ampules inside to mix the chemicals and put a drop on the end of the swab. It immediately turned green.

"Blood. Can't tell ya if it's human or animal, but I'll collect the other spot for further testing."

Mila went back to the boxes. Her heart jumped a little when she came to a gray plastic bin with Amelia's name scrawled in black marker on top. She carefully unsealed the lid and pulled it off. Books, a bunny lamp, and some clothes were what she could see on top. "Hey, P.J., when you're done, I'm gonna need some photos over here."

P.J. carefully photographed each item as Mila lifted it out of the box. She recognized the white dress as the one Amelia was wearing in the painting. When they were done, they returned the items to the box, and Mila carried it out to her SUV.

Garrett was slouched on his porch, drinking his beer and scrolling on his phone. She slammed the liftgate door shut and walked over to him. Sweat rolled between her shoulder blades. She couldn't wait to take a shower. "Want to tell me why you have a box of Amelia's things in your shed?"

"Not really but I will. I can tell you already have your panties in a wad." He grinned and let his eyes wander up and down her body. She fought a shiver. She wouldn't give him the satisfaction of knowing he creeped her out. When she held his stare, he sneered. "We had a garage sale a few years back. Amelia's mom gave me that box to put in there. It just got forgotten when we hauled the leftovers to Goodwill."

"There's also blood on the floor."

He blinked. "Well, probably cut myself in there."

"Then you wouldn't mind giving us a DNA sample to check that?"

He rubbed a meaty hand over the back of his neck. "Jesus, you want my blood?"

"No. Just a simple cheek swab."

He mumbled something under his breath and then threw his hand up. "Fine, but this is bordering on harassment."

Mila nodded, gave him one last look and then walked into the house. Aiden was just coming down the squat set of stairs. She met him at the bottom, taking in the living room. Brown couch with mismatched pillows, cup rings on the coffee table. An underlying smell of old trash. Definitely lacking a woman's touch. "How's it going in here?"

Aiden pulled at the collar of his shirt with a gloved finger. "CSI got some hairs from the spare bedroom and we're taking a camera and a laptop to check. Other than that, I don't see anything pointing to him keeping Amelia here for three years. What about you?"

"Got a few blood drops and a box of Amelia's things. Which Levington says were leftovers from a garage sale." She shrugged.

"Well, he's had a week to clean up after himself."

"Yeah." She checked her Fitbit. They'd been here for three hours. "I'm going to get P.J. to swab Garrett's cheek, write up what we're taking, and then we can get out of here."

※

Mila lay in her bed, the covers flung to the bottom. It was two AM, and she should be getting some much-needed sleep, but her brain wouldn't shut off. Instead, she was scrolling on her phone, looking at everything she could find on Roman Forester. Photos of his art exhibits all over the world, articles about him, interviews with him, photos of him at fancy parties and with celebrities. He was quite the character. Besides female children, he had paintings of ancient goddesses, both beautiful and terrifying. It all felt staged to her, like he was playing a part. Like he kept who he really was carefully hidden behind this elaborate wall he'd constructed. After reading as many articles as she could find, she still had no idea who this man was.

She thought about what her reaction would be if a strange man ever approached her on the beach and asked to paint Harper. It would've been much different than Bobby Sue's. But then again, she's an overprotective cop.

She pinched the screen and enlarged a photo of Roman, dressed in a suit, his curly hair gelled in place and large diamond and emerald earrings catching the flash. His arm was draped over a handsome man who she recognized from the movies but couldn't remember which one.

Who are you when you don't have your public persona mask on, Mr. Forester?

The next day, Mila had to take an actual lunch break to have a conference with Harper's teacher. When she walked up to the office, Paul was waiting for her outside.

"Did you tell Harper about finding Amelia Larson dead?" He was in uniform, smelling like woodsy aftershave, his blue eyes burning bright with anger. This was the side of Paul that those on the other side of the law dealt with.

Mila felt herself go into defensive mode immediately. "Yes, I did. I thought it was better than her hearing it from the other kids."

"Shit, Mila. *You* thought? You didn't think that was possibly a decision to talk to me about? That I'd have some perspective?"

Mila crossed her arms. "No, what I thought was you were busy." She emphasized the word *busy* and spit it from her mouth like poison.

Paul's eyes darkened. He knew what she meant, who she was referring to.

Ms. Piper opened the door, then paused awkwardly when she noticed their stand-off.

"We'll discuss this later," Paul said. Nodding to the slight brunette with glasses, he made an "after you" motion.

Ms. Piper forced a smile and turned, leading them back into the small room. She closed the door then slipped behind her desk and took a seat. Bookshelves stuffed with books and binders bracketed the desk and two plastic chairs sat in front of it. There were no windows.

Mila felt claustrophobic in the small space and wished Ms. Piper had left the door open. Paul's bulky figure radiating heat next to her didn't help.

Ms. Piper folded her pale hands on the desk. "I know you're both busy, so I won't take up too much of your time. I just wanted you to be aware that Harper refused to go outside today. She's really been affected by little Amelia Larson's death."

Mila felt Paul's glare on the side of her face. She ignored him.

"I let her stay in and draw and she drew this." Ms. Piper handed a sheet of 12x18 paper across the desk.

Mila took it and as she processed the images, her hand went to her mouth. *Is this what went on in her daughter's head?*

Paul was silently clenching his jaw beside her as he stared at the drawing.

The drawing was of the school playground, but dead children littered the ground, children with black x's for eyes, scribbles of red blood pooling around their bodies, even some with limbs cut off and hanging from the monkey bars.

"Christ," Paul breathed.

Mila squeezed her eyes shut and dropped the drawing back on the desk.

"She was also upset that her dog was sick and is worried he will die, too."

Paul's head whipped toward Mila. "What happened with Oscar?"

Mila met his furious gaze with her own. "The vet thinks he ate something poisonous. He was pretty sick yesterday, but he's fine now. It's under control."

Paul's brows pressed down in concern, but their attention went back to the teacher when she spoke.

"Honestly, it's probably pretty normal," she said gently. "Harper is a sensitive child, so this doesn't surprise me. But nonetheless, I thought you should know."

"How would you suggest we handle this?" Paul asked.

"Well, I can give you the name of a great children's psychologist. Leigh Ann Pilzner. Wouldn't hurt to have Harper meet with her. Work out some of these overwhelming feelings. She's probably more aware of these things than most children because of your jobs." She dug in her drawer and handed Paul a business card. He glanced down at it. Then over at Mila, brow raised. "Any objections?"

Mila couldn't speak past the guilt squeezing the air from her lungs. She simply shook her head.

When they stepped out of the office, Mila felt numb. She just wanted to find Harper and take her home, hide her from the world.

Paul cleared his throat beside her. "Look, I know you did what you thought was best. Just..." He waited until she looked up at him and offered her a small smile. "Next time, let's talk first, okay?"

He handed her the psychologist's card. "Don't beat yourself up, Mila. You're a great mom."

Mila felt the prickling of tears and had to look away. "I gotta get back to the station. I'll let you know when I make the appointment."

Mila spent the next four hours at the station, following up on leads from the original files.

Aiden had returned from talking to Shelby Myers, and that was a dead end. She didn't remember anything new from the day Amelia Larson disappeared.

Frustrated, Mila began gathering her things. She had planned on going back home for dinner to spend some time with Harper and talk to her.

But at four-fifteen, all hell broke loose.

Nine

Captain Bartol was breathing heavily when she rushed out of her office, slipping her arms into a black blazer and juggling her leather bag. "We got a missing six-year-old girl," she called. "Palm Garden Elementary. Let's go."

Chairs squeaked and rolled as Mila, Aiden and Frank jumped up, grabbed their things and rushed out behind her.

Mila pulled up behind the line of police cars blocking the front of Palm Garden Elementary, blue lights flashing. They belonged to both Edgewater PD and the Pinellas County Sheriff's Department.

She was waved through into the school parking lot. She got as close as she could, slid out of the SUV and headed into the older brick building, which had been retrofitted with new bulletproof glass and doors that required every visitor to be buzzed in.

The front office was packed with uniformed officers taking statements from harried-looking front office women, who had been separated into different corners of the room. Some of them were pressing Kleenex beneath their glasses. Some of them were hugging themselves for comfort.

She glanced back as Captain Bartol, Frank, and Aiden rushed through the door behind her.

Sergeant Lockett came barreling toward them from a side hallway, waving his arm. A man on a mission. They forced their way through the crowd until they reached him.

"Follow me," he grunted, turning and heading back down the hall.

They pushed through double doors and emerged outside, at the back of the school. There were round concrete tables with attached benches arranged in a grassy area to the left. A wide lawn with soccer nets and a small playground beyond that and then a fence. Mila noted it was a simple chain link that hadn't been updated with the new security protocols yet. It backed up to Weeden State Park.

A few uniforms were taping off the fence line.

Mila turned toward the deep sobs coming from one of the tables to their left. She recognized the pain in those sobs. Loss, terror, grief. It must be the mother.

Sergeant Lockett paused beneath the overhang and turned to them, holding up a notebook. "What we know so far. The mother," he pointed behind him with his thumb to the sobbing woman, "Raelynn Parks, was having a teacher conference and let her daughter, Conly Parks age six, play on the playground while they talked. The teacher conference lasted about twenty-five minutes. She came out here to get Conly, and the girl was gone."

"Cameras?" Captain Bartol asked.

He nodded grimly. "Not very good quality. Grainy black and white. But good enough to see the girl follow a drone to the fence line and then a tall figure appearing at the tree line of the park. He helps her over the fence, and they disappear at 4:58 PM."

"Helps her? You mean she went willingly?" Captain Bartol asked.

He nodded, his lips pressed together in a scowl.

Mila cleared her throat. "Someone she knew? Is the father in the picture?"

He shifted on his feet. "Raelynn Parks is a single mom. Conly's dad died of a drug overdose when she was three. No other relatives to speak of. We'll talk to the mother's friends and acquaintances. I've got the office printing out copies of her photo for our LEOs. We'll need to get flyers up ASAP." He turned to Captain Bartol, his expression grim. "I've put a call in to Tampa's Child Abduction Response Team's Special Agent Supervisor. The team should be here within the next two hours."

They all nodded their approval and relief.

The CART team was a multi-agency, multi-jurisdictional response team that had begun in 2004 after a child abduction ended tragically. The preplanning and already trained scalable teams made a world of difference when it came to the first crucial twenty-four hours after a child disappeared. If an abducted child is killed, ninety-one percent of those deaths occur within the first twenty-four hours.

Along with specially trained investigators, there were forensic experts, equipment like all-terrain vehicles, search dogs, helicopters and a mobile command post at the ready. They also had trained civilian volunteers prepared to help search.

"Meanwhile," Sergeant Lockett continued, "I've got our own search and rescue K-9s coming to start on the other side of that fence." They all turned to look across the field. Two of the officers had stopped at a point at the fence, one of them kneeling. That must be the abduction point. "That's a ninety-acre park with five miles of trails. Maybe we'll get lucky and she's still in there."

They glanced at each other. Mila knew they were all thinking the same thing. Children abducted by strangers are more likely to be killed. So, if she is still in there, it probably wasn't a good thing.

"All right." Captain Bartol glanced around, her gaze landing on Mila. "Mila, you talk to Raelynn Parks then take her home. Get as many uniforms as you can to start canvasing her neighborhood, knocking on doors and get a crime scene tech in to process her home." Then she turned to Aiden. "You're in charge of on-scene evidence here. Make sure you get us a copy of that video. Coordinate with the CART team when they get here." She shifted on her feet and looked at Frank. "Get all the names of witnesses and anyone else who had contact with Conly. We'll need a list for Matt to start background checks on. Go ahead and video everyone here, too. We don't know that there's only one person involved in this abduction." She glanced over at the fence line, her face scrunched in thought. "I'll get back and report the case to the National Center for Missing and Exploited Children then get a hotline established for tips and get the 800 number out to the press." She blew out a breath. "Let's get this little girl home alive."

They parted ways with their assignments. Mila assessed Raelynn Parks as she approached the picnic bench where Officer Barb Polanski sat with her. She and Officer Polanski greeted each other with a silent nod.

Raelynn was dressed in a silk baby blue blouse and black pants, her hair and nails looked fresh from the salon, her hands and neck dripping with gold jewelry. She had a wad of Kleenex pressed to her nose, her red-rimmed gaze locked on the officers at the fence line. A purple backpack with butterflies sat on her lap.

Mila motioned to Officer Polanski that she could go, took a seat across from Raelynn and opened her leather notebook. "Ms. Parks?"

The woman's eyes flicked toward Mila, mascara smeared below her lashes. "Yes." She quickly moved her attention back to the officers. She was afraid she'd miss something.

Mila understood, but she needed the woman's attention. She put more urgency in her tone. "Mr. Parks. I'm Detective

Harlow. I'm going to need to ask you a few questions and then take you back home."

"No!" She pulled the backpack protectively into her chest. "I'm not leaving here without my daughter."

"I understand. But we don't know how long the search will go on, and the best way for you to help Conly is to help me gather as much information about her, about the people in her orbit as you can. I'll also need to search her room. Will you help me?"

Panic still rounded the corners of her bloodshot eyes, and her breathing had grown erratic. But she finally seemed to relent. "Okay."

"Thank you." Mila explained about the CART team that was on its way. This seemed to give her a bit of relief. "Let's start with when you left Conly out here to play. Did you see anyone? Any staff? Did anyone else know she was out here?"

She shook her head but then said, "Well, there was a janitor, I think his name's Roberto. He was going into one of the classrooms over there." She pointed to the row of classroom doors behind her. Her hand was visibly shaking. "The one on the end. He waved. We waved back. We've seen him around plenty over the last two years."

Mila scratched that down and then looked up at her expectantly.

"Then I don't know. I told Coco not to get on the monkey bars, to stay on the swings and watched her run to the playground. Came back twenty-five minutes later after talking to her teacher and she was just... gone." A sob broke through again, and Mila gave her a moment to get her emotions back under control.

"That's what you call her? Coco?"

"That's what everyone calls her."

"Okay." Mila asked her to take her through their day starting with when they left the house. Nothing unusual had happened. Though to Mila it seemed like someone would have had to have been stalking the little girl, already had her in their crosshairs. Otherwise, how would a twenty-five-minute window be enough to get through Weeden Park, set up on the other side of the fence and grab her? "And do you have any idea who Coco would feel comfortable enough to leave with? A family friend? A friend's parent?"

"I mean, as much as we talked about stranger danger, she was an outgoing child. She talked to everyone. Loved to entertain people, try to make them laugh."

"She sounds like a great kid. What was she wearing today?"

"Purple leggings, white shirt with a sparkly smiley face and white sneakers."

Mila eyed the backpack and glanced over at the officer, motioning her over. "I'm going to ask you to leave the backpack with Officer Polanski here. They'll bring in search dogs and will need something with Coco's scent to track."

Mila asked her a few more questions, took notes and then stood. "Let's go back to your house. You can leave your car here and ride with me."

She texted Aiden to talk to the janitor, Roberto, and then stopped by the office to pick up some copies of Coco's photo. Mila stared at the smiling girl with dark brown eyes, black spiral curls, and a dimple on her right cheek. She was a beautiful child with a joyful spirit. Mila silently hoped the monster who took her wouldn't snuff that out.

In the parking lot, now swarming with more police cars and press, Raelynn pointed to a silver Mercedes. "I have to get my things." Mila followed her and waited while she grabbed a leather computer bag and a gym bag from the back seat. The car still had that new car leather smell.

Mila glanced behind her at the press vans. Elly Prescott's affiliate station was there, but no sign of her. She was probably already in the office, finding the most vulnerable male officer she could sink her teeth into. She noticed officers putting up barriers and tape around the perimeter of the school.

When they were seated in Mila's SUV, she asked Raelynn for the address, plugged it into her GPS and they were on their way. It was only going to be a seven-minute drive. Mila called dispatch and asked for a crime scene tech and as many uniforms as they could spare to meet her at the address as she made a left next to a mobile home park. She noticed some roof damage on a line of trailers from the hurricane. Or maybe from a tornado spawned by the storm. Those sometimes did more damage.

Raelynn's house was two neighborhoods back, in a well-established but not wealthy part of Edgewater. As she cruised through the street and around a bend, eyeing the small houses with weedy yards and junk cars in the driveway, she couldn't help thinking how out of place Raelynn's Mercedes would look here.

"How long have you and Coco lived here?" she asked as she bumped over a large crack in the cement drive and parked.

"I've lived here for fourteen years," she said, glancing at the house before gathering her belongings. "It was my dad's. I inherited it when he passed, along with all the expenses, and me and Darnell didn't have much when we got married." Her voice was like a robot. Mila wondered if she was disassociating or going into shock. "I've been working with a real estate agent to find a better neighborhood, but the home prices are insane right now."

Mila couldn't argue with that. This neighborhood may look shabby, but she knew there was little crime here. A car broken into once in a while, a domestic disturbance. Nothing that would've put Coco in close proximity to unsavory characters like drug dealers. Matt would check the sex offender registry though.

A patrol car rolled up and parked alongside the road as Raelynn was unlocking the door. Mila watched two more units rounding the bend behind that one. Raelynn paused and took a shaky breath. "I can't believe I'm coming home without her," she whispered. "This feels like a fucking nightmare that I can't wake up from."

It is a nightmare. Every parent's worst nightmare in fact.

Mila didn't say it though. Instead, she squeezed Raelynn's arm gently. "There will be hundreds of people tearing this town apart looking for her very soon. I promise." Mila waved as the officers began exiting their vehicles.

Raelynn nodded and pushed the house door open.

Mila adjusted her leather satchel on her shoulder and followed.

"Where do you want me to wait?" Raelynn looked lost in her own house.

"Here in the living room is fine. I'm just going to take a quick look around."

Two officers walked through the still-opened door as Raelynn lowered herself on the sofa. She lifted a child-sized blanket from the couch, adorned with Cinderella figures, and sat frozen, clutching the blanket to her chest and staring out the window.

The officers approached Mila and introduced themselves. One was a Sergeant. "We doin' door knocks?"

"Yeah. We're particularly interested in any observations about strangers in the neighborhood, unknown cars parked in the area, if Coco interacted with anyone or anyone took an interest in her. Also, I want the license plate of any car that drives down this road from now on." She reached into her bag, pulled out a handful of the copied photos of Coco, and offered them to him. If these aren't enough, snap a photo and text it to the other officers. "Sergeant Borek, I'm going to need you to stay here with Ms. Parks."

"Not a problem." He moved back to the door where the other officers were waiting, throwing Raelynn a sympathetic glance on his way out.

Mila stood, taking in the house for a moment, getting a first impression. It was messy but not dirty. The cream tile floors were clean, outdated white kitchen counters were cluttered but no dishes in the sink. Pictures, obviously drawn by a child, hung on the fridge.

Mila stepped into the kitchen and looked closer at the pictures. A brown beach, blue water and a large yellow sun dominated them. A stick child and woman holding hands with large smiles. A happy child. Mila pushed aside the images of blood and death her own child had drawn.

She made her way through the house, looking but not touching anything. When the CSI tech got there, she'd video it. She found Coco's room on the right of the squat hallway.

Stepping in, she stood and soaked in the details. Typical girl's room with princess décor, including a canopy bed, purple duvet with gold castles and blue clouds. A huge, framed Disney Frozen poster took up the wall beside the bed. There was a small white vanity to the left, between the wall and closet. Mila walked over to it and slipped on gloves. It was full of baskets of make-up, hair accessories and plastic jewelry. Seemed excessive for a six-year-old. She opened the closet door. It was stuffed with clothes and shoes, but what attracted her attention was the row of princess crowns on the shelf. Her eyes narrowed.

Could this case be connected to the Amelia Larson case? Would the kidnapper take another child now that Amelia was dead?

She'd have to think about that later. Right now, she needed to focus so she didn't miss anything right in front of her. She carefully searched the dresser and nightstand drawers. Finding a diary, she opened it and flipped through the pages. Just some more happy drawings. She got on the floor and looked under the bed. A few stuffed animals and a plastic box with extra bed clothes. She lifted the mattress, moved the pillows. Nothing. Nothing secret or hidden that would suggest someone had been communicating with her.

She returned to the living room in time to let Brooklyn, the ME tech, in the door. Brooklyn had been the one who'd slipped Amelia's birthday crown into a brown evidence bag at the crime scene.

Mila pulled off her gloves and led the young woman to Coco's bedroom. As Brooklyn pushed her glasses up and glanced around the room, Mila said, "Get me her fingerprints and hair samples. Collect her toothbrush, too. We'll need DNA."

"You got it."

Mila nodded her thanks and went back to the living room. She lowered herself onto the sofa next to Raelynn, who hadn't moved. "Ms. Parks?"

The distraught mother turned to Mila, her eyes haunted.

"Did Coco have a cell phone?"

"No," she croaked.

"So, no access to the internet?"

Raelynn's eyes widened. She squeezed the blanket harder and shook her head, but she didn't look convinced.

Mila's mouth pursed in thought. "Is there any reason for someone to believe they could take her for ransom? Do you have a large savings someone could know about?"

At this, Raelynn swallowed hard and turned her body toward Mila, still clutching the blanket like it was a life raft saving her from drowning. "Maybe. There is something you should know." A flash of guilt turned into fear. Her jaw trembled as she said, "About two weeks ago a man found Coco. I don't know how because I don't even use her real name and never give out her location."

Mila held up her hand. "What do you mean 'found her'?"

There was that flash of guilt again. "Well… it's better if I show you." She dug into the bag at her feet and pulled out a cell phone. After a few swipes, she held the phone out to Mila. "I run an Instagram account for her. It started as just fun. Like when she'd make funny videos singing or whatever. But then we started getting offers from brands for her to wear their clothes or try their products."

Mila glanced over the profile. Over a million followers. *Holy shit.* She scrolled through the photos and noticed a lot of videos of her in bathing suits on the beach.

"We make an insane amount of money off it through sponsors and the creative fund. So, yes, I do have quite a bit in a savings account for her college. But who could know that?"

Mila sent the link to herself and then handed Raelynn back her phone. "You said this guy found her. Did you report it?"

"Oh yes. I have a doorbell camera, so I had a clear shot of him. The police interviewed him. He apparently lives in Tampa."

Mila made a note to look up the police report and get this guy's name.

"That's never happened before," Raelynn said. "It did scare me, and I was considering taking the account down. I just haven't yet."

A firecracker of anger popped in Mila's chest. *Of course not, because then how could she afford her new Mercedes?* She handed Raelynn her notepad and pen. "I'm going to need you to write down the names and numbers of Coco's close friends and yours."

She watched as Raelynn pulled up numbers on her cell phone and wrote them down with a shaky hand.

Mila explained to her how once the word gets out, she may get calls from strangers, psychics, threats, etc. "In case you do receive a call from someone claiming to be involved in

Coco's abduction, you need to think of something that only you and Coco would know to verify they have her."

"Um. She had a hamster that died last year. His name was Rufus."

"That's good. You ask the name, use that as proof if they say they have your daughter." Mila jotted that down. "Sergeant Borek is going to stay with you. We're going to get your carrier to set up a trap and trace on your cell in case this is a kidnapping for ransom and you receive any communication from the perp. We'll be able to see the location of any callers." She pulled out her card and laid it on the coffee table. "I'm going to go follow up on the report you filed. See if I can find out where this guy is right now. There will be a victim advocate coming to talk to you soon, but call me if you need anything." Mila saw the panic creeping in, stiffening the woman's body.

She knelt and took Raelynn's hand between her own, her voice softening. "Look, Raelynn, I have a daughter, too. I understand how scared you are right now, but I promise you, we are going to do everything in our power to bring Coco back home." She almost said *alive*, but she tried not to make promises she couldn't keep.

Raelynn choked back a sob as she nodded.

Mila left the distraught mom clutching the blanket and her cell phone. Her body had begun to shake like she was starting to thaw from the shock. The best thing Mila could do for her was to go find her daughter.

After calling Sergeant Lockett and briefing him on what she needed his officers to be doing, she let Captain Bartol know she was following up on the guy who found Coco on Instagram. The one who showed up at the Parks's house.

Mila pulled up the incident report Raelynn filed two weeks ago and read through it. Steven Shaw, age thirty-two of Tampa, Florida. He'd knocked on the door. Raelynn had opened it and he'd presented a bouquet of roses, asked if he could give them to Coco and meet her. When Raelynn had tried to shut the door, he'd stuck his foot in the door to stop her. He'd repeated his request, but more forcefully. Raelynn had kicked him in the kneecap, causing him to move his foot, and she was then able to close the door and call the police. He had left but police were able to identify him through the ring cam footage. He was interviewed, but there were no charges brought. He agreed not to approach Raelynn or her daughter again.

She pulled up the address. It was an apartment in Tampa. She hit the gas.

TEN

Mila rapped her knuckles hard on the door and waited. The door opened and she swept her gaze over the thin man with a goatee standing in front of her. Two hours had passed since Coco had disappeared. Could this man have taken her, stashed her somewhere and ended up back at home in that time? Yes, it was possible, but was it plausible? His demeanor was calm and curious. Besides the slight surprise of seeing a stranger at his door, he didn't look nervous.

"Steven Shaw?" she asked.

"Yeah?"

She pushed her blazer jacket aside and let him see her badge. "Detective Harlow Edgewater PD. I need to ask you a few questions about the incident with Coco Parks."

His head dropped. "Look, I haven't gone anywhere near the girl since that day. I swear."

"So you wouldn't mind letting me take a look around your apartment?"

He cocked his head. "My apartment? Why?"

"Coco went missing two hours ago from her school." She carefully watched his reaction.

"Missing?" He looked at her with wide, horror-filled eyes. "Jesus. I'm sorry to hear that." He stroked his goatee then sighed and waved her in. "My lawyer would kick my ass for this but do what you need to do. I don't have anything to hide."

Mila stepped inside. "Can you have a seat on the sofa while I take a look, please?"

He sat, muted the TV, and reached for a can of Miller Light on the coffee table.

Mila swept the apartment quickly. One bedroom, one bathroom, pantry in the kitchen. Not many places to hide a child, but that didn't mean he was innocent. He could've already killed and dumped her somewhere.

She returned to the living room and stood across from him. "Tell me about your day. What did you do?"

He pressed his back into the sofa and looked up at her. His eyes were narrowed but more out of concentration than anger. "I was at work until 4:30, then stopped by Publix to grab a Pub Sub. Got home around sixish." His mouth turned up at one corner. "Not a very exciting life, I'm afraid."

She pulled a small notebook out of her blazer pocket. "Where do you work?"

He gave her the name and phone number. She jotted that down and then asked, "Do you still have the Publix receipt?"

He rubbed his hands on his jeans. "Ah, yeah. Probably." He got up and pulled the lid off the kitchen trash can, sending a waft of old food smell her way. Digging in the can, he lifted the receipt and brought it to her. She didn't touch it. There was a large grease stain on it. But she read the time stamp. 4:53 PM. His alibi held. She snapped a photo of it.

"Thank you," she said, pocketing her phone. "Why did you show up at Coco's house that day?"

He sat back down and picked up his beer. Looking at her sheepishly, he said, "I have a daughter her age. She lives in Michigan with her mother, and I haven't seen her in a year. Honestly, I wasn't trying to be a creep. I guess I just got caught up in the fantasy that I knew Coco from following her on Instagram." He shrugged. "Looking back, it was stupid. I just wanted to give her something nice. Something that I couldn't give my daughter. I miss her."

Mila didn't buy it. Why was he following a six-year-old girl on social media in the first place? But it didn't matter right now. He didn't seem to be the present danger. "How did you find Coco's address?"

"The photos her mother posts, they don't have the location turned off. I'm actually surprised no one else has showed up at her door yet." His head jerked up. "Or maybe they just showed up at her school."

A chill crawled up Mila's spine. *Is that how the kidnapper found her?* "Thank you for your time, Mr. Shaw."

"I really hope you find her and she's okay," he said.

"Me too." She stopped at the door and turned back. "One more thing. Where did you live three years ago?'"

"Here. Been here for almost five years now."

Mila nodded, but her mind was already racing. They would have to check Coco's other IG followers. A million of them. Matt was going to have a long few nights.

When she returned to her SUV, she immediately pulled up her phone, clicked the link she'd sent herself, and opened Coco's Instagram account. She hit "followers" and began to scroll. Her mood darkened as her eyes scanned the profiles of the little girl's followers. They were mostly grown men.

"What the hell?" Backing out of "followers" she scrolled through Coco's images. Two weeks ago there were videos of Coco eating things like popsicles and pickles. Looks like Raelynn had at least stopped posting that garbage after Steven Shaw found her. Mila threw her phone into her bag with a growl of disgust and strangled the steering wheel.

How could Raelynn not see the danger? Was she that naive? Or was she just blinded by the money?

Shaking her head, Mila started the engine and headed back to Edgewater.

Garden Park Elementary was now surrounded by law enforcement vehicles, their red and blue lights chewing up the darkness. She stopped at the barricade, her gaze sweeping the parking lot. There were at least four counties present that she could count.

An incident command center tent had been set up and a crowd of people in red jackets milled around it. She knew these were the search and rescue volunteers. There was also a group of men in camo pants and khaki shirts with "K-9" on the back. One of them had a Malinois and one had a black Lab on a long lead. CART had arrived.

She turned her SUV around and cut through the back street to Weeden State Park. She knew Captain Bartol was back at the station, but she wanted to see if they'd found anything on the other side of the fence. Parking along the road, she walked to the officer holding the clipboard and signed her name and badge number.

Once inside the parking lot, she spotted two members of Paul's Clearwater PD K-9 team, Jackson and Mateo. They were like brothers to Paul. She headed for them, rubbing her lower back, which was strained from the drive to Tampa.

Mateo noticed her first as she made her way around a group of volunteers. He held up a hand in greeting.

She approached, and he gave her a one-arm hug. His dog, a black shepherd named Riggs, glanced at her but then his attention went back to the trees at the edge of the park. "*Hola, Amiga.* Long time no see."

Jackson greeted her, too. His K-9, Chevy, must be in the patrol car. "Not the best circumstances."

"No, it's not." She glanced over at the entrance of the path leading into the woods, where Sargeant Lockett was talking with a group of sheriff's deputies and the ME tech, P.J. Mila would recognize that red ponytail anywhere. "They got anything yet?"

Mateo shook his head. "Three separate dogs have all followed the trail from the point of abduction to the south path and right to the parking lot. The scent disappears here."

"He took her by car," Mila said. Coco could be anywhere by now. "Well, that means she was probably alive when she left the park at least." Finding her body in the woods would have been worse news. She glanced around. "No cameras in the parking lot?"

"Nope," Jackson answered. "Two trail cams, though. One caught 'em and they also got a witness. Homeless guy camping in the woods. I saw Detective Reyes leading him away, so I'm assuming he took him to Edgewater PD for the interview."

Aiden. "Good. A witness is good." She turned to go and then glanced back. "Hey, thanks for the sandbags during Henry. I owe you guys a BBQ."

Jackson rubbed the back of his muscular neck. "We find this little girl alive, and we'll throw an all-out party."

"Yes, we will," Mila agreed. "Take care."

Mila poked her head into the Edgewater PD media room around 8:30 PM. The room was normally used for holding big press conferences, but the large space with long tables and two giant monitors mounted on the front wall also made a great staging area when multiple jurisdictions were involved.

Tonight it was packed with people, but she didn't see Captain Bartol or Aiden. She greeted Francine, their front office admin, and then swiped her badge to enter the secured inner workings of the department, making her way to the bullpen.

The room was hectic. The steady hum of voices, punctuated by ringing phones, added to the chaos as she tried to find one of her teammates. She spotted Captain Bartol heading into her office with two men in suits and ties trailing behind her. She'd have to wait until their meeting was over to brief the captain about what she'd learned so far.

Frank was on the phone at his desk. A young woman had a chair pulled up beside it and was writing in a notepad. Aiden wasn't at his desk, so she went and checked the monitor where they could watch the interview rooms. All three rooms were occupied. Matt sat in his wheelchair in front of an elderly woman in Room Three, taking notes.

Room One held Aiden and a man wearing layers of clothing, his face obscured by a heavy white beard and a dirty, torn backpack at his feet. This must be the witness from the park. Mila slipped on a pair of headphones to block out the noise in the bullpen and pushed a button on the computer to listen in on Room One.

"You've been a big help, Dirks. Can I get you to sit with a sketch artist? Maybe try to come up with something for us to give the media?"

Dirks scratched his thick gray beard with dirty fingers. "I mean, I can try. But like I said, I didn't see his face. He had a hoodie on, and I was really paying attention to the little girl. It seemed odd to see a grown man walking a little girl through the park that way. She didn't seem in no distress though. He was holding her hand and in her other hand was a Barbie doll she was paying attention to." He shrugged. "The man never looked my way."

Mila's stomach sank. No ID. Damn. The Barbie must've been how he lured her over to the fence. What about the trail cam? Jackson had mentioned it caught them. Maybe they'd get something from that.

Aiden was looking over his notes. "Just to be clear, you stated you did not see the man favoring one leg or limping?"

"Nope."

Mila frowned and immediately thought of Roman Forester. *Why did Aiden ask that question?* She was about to find out. Aiden pushed his chair back and told Mr. Dirks to stay put.

Mila removed the headphones as Aiden came through the back door and headed toward her.

"Hey, give me one sec," he said as he passed her.

She turned and followed him back to his desk.

He plopped in his chair and snatched up the phone receiver. "I need a sketch artist here in the bullpen ASAP." He replaced the receiver and turned his chair toward Mila, raking a hand down his face. "What do you have for me?"

She handed him her notebook. "These are Raelynn and Coco's closest friends."

He snapped a photo of the list and nodded. "Thanks. I'll get patrol to pick them up next." He reached into his desk drawer, pulled out a brown paper bag, and handed it to her. "Paige brought some sandwiches if you're feeling brave. They're grilled veggies and hummus."

Mila took it with a grateful nod. She'd learned not to be picky. Who knew when they'd get to eat next? "One day you'll have to tell me how you convinced her to marry you." After taking a bite and forcing herself to swallow, she asked, "Why did you ask the witness about a limp?"

Aiden chugged half a bottle of water and then glanced up like he'd forgotten something. "You haven't seen the trail cam footage." He didn't wait for an answer. Just turned back around and wiggled his mouse to bring his monitor to life. "Matt made us a copy of this and the footage of the abduction, so we could study it for anything missed."

Grabbing her desk chair with the hand that wasn't holding the sandwich, she rolled it up beside his as he pulled up the footage. "This is the abduction footage. Black and white and grainy but you can clearly see Coco notice the drone with something dangling from it."

"The Barbie doll." The bite she'd just taken got caught behind the lump in her throat.

"Yep."

They continued to watch as Coco followed the drone right up to the fence line. A person in a hoodie was crouching down behind it. The little girl blocked their view of him for about thirty seconds and then she lifted her arms up. So trusting. Did she know the person?

Mila wanted to scream at her to run like she could stop this from happening.

He reached and lifted her over the fence, and they disappeared into the trees in the next second. Just like that. A little girl gone.

Mila's heart was thudding like a hollow drum in her chest. Her fight or flight response had kicked in, a thin sheen of sweat chilling her skin.

Aiden scanned her face with concern. "I know that was hard to watch. You okay?"

She wrapped up the remaining few bites of her sandwich, no longer able to swallow. "Yeah. Let's see the trail cam." Her voice was tight in a constricted throat, but she ignored her distress.

The trail cam picked up the two of them coming around a bend in the trail. Coco was focused on the doll in her hand. The perp was clutching her other hand. A black or dark gray oversized hoodie hid his body and face, and he wore jeans and work boots. At one point, parallel to the camera, he reached up and adjusted the hoodie and a few curls slipped out. Again, the footage was in black and white, so it was hard to tell what color the hair was. But what caught Mila's attention was the slight limp the man had.

"That's why you asked the witness about the limp. Can you freeze it there?" She studied the man's posture. "Roman Forester has curly hair and a slight limp like that. But why wouldn't Dirks notice that?"

Aiden shrugged. "You know how witness testimony is. Not accurate or reliable, especially when we have a video that contradicts it."

Mila stared at the image frozen on the screen. "Those aren't clothes Roman Forester would have in his wardrobe or be caught dead in."

"A disguise to throw us off. Could've picked them up from Goodwill."

She leaned forward, taking in every detail of the kidnapper. "Say it is Roman Forester. Why would Coco go with him so willingly? Did she know him? And do we think her case is connected to Amelia's?"

Aiden stared at the screen, pulling at his bottom lip. Then he smacked the desk and looked at her with a raised brow. "Maybe he painted her, too. Let's find out."

Mila nodded, looked up her notes for Raelynn's cell phone and dialed. When Raelynn's shaky voice answered, Mila identified herself. "Do you know a man named Roman Forester? Or has Coco ever come in contact with him that you know of?"

"The artist. Yeah." Her tone was flat, exhausted. "He approached us a few weeks ago at the farmer's market. Gave me his card and asked if he could paint Coco. I never contacted him, though. Figured he'd want too much money, being famous and all. Wait. You think he took Coco?"

"Just looking into every possibility right now. Thank you." She blew out a breath as she disconnected. Nodding, she told Aiden, "He noticed Coco and gave Raelynn his card. I'll go have another chat with him. Get his whereabouts at the time of the abduction."

Just then, Captain Bartol walked out of her office with the two men and spotted Mila. All three of them wore grim expressions as they approached.

"Update?" the captain asked.

Mila filled her in on everything she'd found out and told her she was going to go talk to Roman Forester again.

Captain Bartol crossed her arms, clearly not liking the idea. "Be careful. He's got powerful allies in this town, and we've only got one shot at him. Wait until morning and keep it friendly." She turned to Aiden and introduced the two men, detectives from Clearwater who were going to help interview witnesses.

Aiden shook hands with the men. "Great. I've got a list of the family's close friends. Let's get them in here."

Mila spotted Matt coming out of the interview room. She maneuvered around the extra bodies to get to him. "Hey, Matt, I need to show you Coco's Instagram account."

His dark brows raised, and he jerked his head, signaling her to follow him to his office.

Once he rolled up to his desk and looked at her expectantly, she closed the door, grateful for the silence, and pulled up Coco's IG account on her phone. "The mother runs this account for Coco." She handed the phone to Matt and watched as he scrolled, his expression darkening.

"Over a million followers? And let me guess…" His voice was raw with emotion as the screen lit up his face. "Yep… mostly grown men. Fuck."

He let the phone drop into his lap and swiped a hand down his face. Then he pulled up the account on his computer monitor and shook his head. "I can make a list of frequent commenters to start, but this will be too much of a time suck for one person. The FBI has offered their help. Think I'm going to have to give this to them."

Mila nodded. "I wonder…" She opened the search bar in IG and typed in Roman's name. There was one verified account: Roman_artist. "Can you check if this account has made any comments on her posts?" She turned the phone, and Matt jotted down the account name.

"Sure thing."

Around 10:30 PM, Mila stepped out of interview Room Three after talking with one of Raelynn's work friends to find Matt dropping something off at her desk. "Hey, what's up?"

His dark eyes were rimmed red from staring at the computer screen for hours. "I found one comment from that account on Coco's photo. Printed it out for you."

"Thanks." Mila picked up the paper. The post was a photo of Coco in a strawberry red bikini, caught mid-air jumping over a wave, her light brown eyes glowing, spiral curls like a halo around her head. There were over a hundred thousand likes and hundreds of comments. Roman_artist's comment was highlighted:

Fierce innocence frozen in time. If only it were that simple. A crown emoji followed the comment.

A cold chill ran through Mila as her mind flashed on the birthday crown found by Amelia's body. Was this just a coincidence? Was she trying too hard to tie these cases together?

What are the facts, Mila? What facts link these two girls?

They were both six-year-olds. That was it, nothing else. She hated that their investigation into Amelia's death was getting pushed aside, but the kidnapping had to be a priority. Maybe they could get one girl back alive.

She fell into her chair, suddenly aware of the bone-deep exhaustion and the fog moving over her thoughts until she could barely put two together. She needed sleep, but coffee would have to do. First, she checked her messages.

Kittie had sent her a video of Harper tucked in bed, Oscar stretched over her legs as Harper blew the phone a kiss and said, "Goodnight, Mom. I miss you."

"Good night, sweet girl." Mila sighed. "I miss you, too." She was glad to see Oscar back in his rightful place on the bed.

There was also a text from Paul: *Harper's class went ok. She seems more interested in making friends than learning to defend herself. Tho thought she was gonna kick that Joey kid in the balls when he cut in front of her. Hope ur having a good night.*

He didn't mention Detective Scott again. Good, *she* wouldn't have to kick him in the balls the next time she saw him.

And speaking of the devil. A text from Detective Scott came in: *Let me know if there's anything I can do to help.*

Mila thought about it. She really hadn't gotten a chance to go over Amelia's case with him. What if she was missing something that did connect the two cases? There also wasn't anything she could do at the station this late.

With a decision made, she texted him back: *You up?*

Yep.

Want to take a ride to Odessa with me? See if Garrett Levington has an alibi for today? I can pick you up.

The three dots indicated he was typing. She waited. Finally, just a simple *OK* with his address came through. She would've loved to know what he'd typed and erased. Was he going to make up an excuse but changed his mind?

Grabbing her leather bag and Glock, she went to find Captain Bartol and let her know where she was going. Knocking, she entered her office.

"Hey, Mila. What's up?" She briefly glanced up from whatever she was reading on her laptop. Her red hair stood up in spikes in front like she'd obsessively run her hand through it, and she had on her reading glasses.

Mila glanced around the usually neat office. It looked like a tornado had blown through it and smelled like stale burgers. Bags of takeout food overflowed her metal trash bin, which was also unusual, considering her wife, Brigette, was a former pastry chef and loved to bring her homemade food. The captain was stress-eating.

Mila knew better than to comment though. "I'm going to take a ride out to Odessa, see if Garrett Levington will talk to me."

Captain Bartol frowned, pulling off her reading glasses and finally looking at Mila. "Alone?"

"No. Detective Scott is going to go with me. Figured I can pick his brain on the way."

She leaned back in her chair, blowing out a long breath then nodded. "All right. Go home and catch a few hours of sleep after that, then visit Forester when the sun comes up."

"Yes, ma'am."

Mila grabbed two coffees from the gas station and then followed the GPS to Detective Scott's house. It was about a fifteen-minute drive inland, past a "Pine Acres" sign and into an established neighborhood. The houses themselves were ranch-style, probably built in the seventies and nestled in the brush and trees with at least an acre each. It was peaceful and nice to see the conservation of large swaths of natural habitat. Now when they built in Florida, they just leveled everything and stuck houses a few feet from each other.

As Mila steered into the driveway and her headlights swept across the front of his house, Detective Scott exited, pulling the door shut behind him. He was clad in dark jeans, a black collared shirt and a light jacket that she assumed was covering a gun holster.

He slid into the passenger seat, bringing the scent of leather and aftershave with him. His eyes met hers, and there was a darkness there that prickled her skin before he masked it. It had the same quality of pain she'd watched flash in his eyes at the Beachside Beat. He had been through something brutal and life-changing. She was sure of it.

She offered him a soft smile as she put the SUV in reverse. "Brought you a coffee. Also, you get bonus points for not insisting on driving."

A rough chuckle vibrated in his chest as he reached for the coffee. "Control freak. Got it."

This time it was Mila who chuckled as she found her way back out onto State Road 19.

They drove a few miles with only the low drone of the tires on the asphalt and a country song on the radio breaking the silence.

Then Detective Scott turned from the window. "Does this mean you think the Larson and Parks cases are related?"

She lifted a shoulder, smoothly steering the SUV around a tight bend in the road. "No. I don't know. Maybe. It doesn't matter what I think, it matters what the evidence points to, but I guess if I can rule out the number one suspect in the Amelia Larson case, it makes it easier to narrow the focus." She sighed. "Makes it easier to focus on the number two suspect, who also has a connection to Coco Parks."

"Forester?"

She heard the hope in his voice. "Yep."

"Did he paint Coco's portrait, too?"

"No, but he did give her mother his card and offer to. Also, he follows her on Instagram. Coco, not the mother. Pull up Instagram and search for Coco Parks."

The full moon caught Mila's eye as she cruised down State Road 19. A large, creamy disk in a star-filled sky. Beautiful but a million miles away, just like any answers they may have about these little girls' fates.

A pained grunt came from the man beside her as he laid his phone face down on his knee and pinched the spot between his eyes.

Mila gave him a minute to grapple with the anger they'd all felt after seeing it. Then she said, "Forester left a comment on one of her photos. With a crown emoji. I know it's a stretch, but it made me think of the birthday crown that was left with Amelia Larson's body. Did you run across anything in your investigation that would explain that crown? Why it was left with her?"

His fist opened and closed a few times before he finally rested it on his knee. "No. It wasn't even close to her birthday. She didn't have it when she was abducted."

Mila's lips twisted in disappointment. "Did you hear there's trail cam video from the park? And a witness? A homeless man."

Surprise changed the pitch of his voice when he asked, "A witness?"

She glanced at him. "Yeah, but don't get your hopes up. The witness didn't see any more than the camera did."

"Which was?"

"One man, about six foot in old clothes and a hoodie. Curly hair. The camera caught a limp, but the witness didn't see it."

"Doesn't Forester have a limp?"

"Yep. But not sure he would be caught dead in an old, ragged hoodie."

"Just the thing he'd use to throw us off then."

Mila nodded in agreement. "I'm going to have another friendly chat with him in the morning. See if he has an alibi for Coco's abduction. He's an odd duck, just not sure if he's dangerous."

He lifted his coffee from the cup holder. "He give you anything when you talked to him about Amelia?"

She sighed. "Just talked about how he'd never hurt a little girl because he's a feminist."

Detective Scott went quiet for a minute. "Well, I don't like the fact that her body was dumped right across the bay from his mansion. He has a boat, I'm sure."

"A big one, yeah," Mila said.

After a while, she turned onto the dirt road that led to Garrett Levington's property. "We're waiting on forensics from our search the other day. Found a box of Amelia's things in his garage and a few spots of blood."

His sudden gaze warmed her face. "How did you get a search warrant?"

"The girlfriend, Brenda. She got married, so it's Brenda Gorski now. She caved and admitted she lied about being with him." Mila's mouth quirked up on one side. "And a judge in a good mood." She shut off the SUV, the engine clicking loudly in the darkness as they eyed the house. No porch light, no inside lights on.

"I don't see a car." Detective Scott's deep voice held disappointment.

"No." Mila opened the car door, flooding them with the interior light. "But we came all this way. Might as well knock."

Pulling out her flashlight, Mila swept it over the grounds and then the porch before she climbed the steps and rapped on the door with the end of it. It was a still night, no breeze, so the air felt thick and clingy. They waited. Detective Scott was a welcomed presence at her shoulder. She pounded on the door again, this time harder. "Mr. Levington, open up. Edgewater PD."

To their surprise, it opened and a visibly drunk Garrett Levington stood there in nothing but a pair of blue boxers, squinting at them.

"Oh, you," he snarled. "What the fuck do you want?" His glassy, bloodshot eyes narrowed. "Forget to search my ass? Well, go on then." He made a show of turning and tried to bend over but stumbled and fell against the wall. "Shit," he slurred.

Mila and Detective Scott shared a look. Amused but wary. Drunks could be unpredictable. "Mr. Levington, we just need to ask you a few questions about your whereabouts today."

He was leaning hard against the door frame, looking at Mila like she'd just told him aliens had landed in his yard. "You needed to know this right now. In the middle of the night? Why?" His gaze suddenly focused on Detective Scott. "Wait a damn minute. I know you." His face reddened and his lips parted, baring clenched teeth. "My lawyer already told you I don't have a damn thing to say to you. Get the fuck off my property."

Mila turned to Detective Scott and gave him a slight nod. They needed this man calm.

Detective Scott leaned into her, his warm breath sending goosebumps down her arms as he rumbled, "Gonna take a look around."

She cleared her throat and stifled her body's traitorous reaction. Maybe it was time she started dating. "He's gone. It's just me." She gave Garrett Levington her most disarming smile, watching as his shoulders relaxed. "I'm going to be honest with you, Garrett. May I call you Garrett?"

His eyes narrowed with suspicion, but he gave a nod as he leaned harder on the door frame, a waft of stale beer emanating from his pores.

She held her hands out in front of her. "I really didn't want to bother you this late. But another girl is missing, so I just need to cross you off our suspect list. You understand, right?" She nodded and he nodded along. "So, just tell me where you were today, and we can leave you to get back to your evening."

He dug the edge of his palm into his eye, rubbing hard. "I worked 'til two then came home and watched the Jet's game."

Mila peered into the dark living room behind him, straining to hear any noise, any sign there was another soul in the house. "Alone?"

His tongue darted out and wet his bottom lip as he smirked. "Yeah, you offering to remedy that?"

Mila ignored his attempt to get a rise out of her. Instead, she cocked her head and held his stare. "You know, if you really want us to leave you alone, you'd explain the Christmas ham comment you made to your brother from prison."

He was just drunk enough to take the bait. "For fuck's sake," he exploded, spittle hitting her face. She wiped it off with the back of her hand, keeping her expression neutral. "It was about my boat, okay? They were tryin' to repo my boat, and I had my brother hide it until I could catch up on payments." He wobbled as he pushed off the doorframe. "Happy?"

Mila studied him. "I'd be happier if you let me take a look inside."

"No fuckin' way, lady. Unless you got one of them papers you brought last time." The anger simmered. "You can kindly fuck off now." He slammed the door in her face, and she could still hear him cussing at her behind the door.

She smirked and flicked her flashlight back on. Crossing the yard, she found Detective Scott lifting the tarp on the small boat beside the shed and running the beam of his flashlight across the deck.

"Find anything?" she asked, coming up behind him.

He dropped the tarp and rested a hand on his hip. "No sign of the girl. The shed's padlocked, but I knocked on all the walls and didn't get a response. You get anything from him?"

"He said he worked until two PM and then was home alone watching the Jet's game."

Detective Scott's eyes glistened as he calculated something in his head. "That gives him enough time to drive to Edgewater."

"Yeah, we'll keep him on the list for now." Though her gut was telling her he didn't make that drive.

They walked back through the yard to the SUV in silence.

After a few minutes on the road, Mila felt the heavy weight of sleep pulling at her eyelids. She took a few mouthfuls of the cold coffee, but it wasn't even touching the bone-deep exhaustion. "Tell me about yourself, Detective. I need to stay awake."

He shifted his body, adjusted himself in the seat so he could look at her. "Afraid that'd put you to sleep. Nothing much exciting to tell." Behind his declaration lay a somber shadow, the tone contradicting the words.

It made her more curious. She glanced over at him. "Everyone's got a story. Where'd you grow up? Any family? Nerd or jock?"

His prickly silence made her more aware of the steady road noise beneath the tires. Just when she thought he was going to ignore her, he said, "Talking will keep you awake better than listening. You go first."

A low sound of disappointment rumbled in her throat. Just like Paul, more interested in putting up that wall, not letting anyone in.

Stop thinking about Paul.

Sneaking another glance at him, a tingling sensation fluttered in her core when her gaze snagged on his eyes shining in the dark. She tamped it down. Definitely needed to start dating.

"All right, you win. I grew up in Sarasota but spent summers in Edgewater with my grandmother and siblings. Two brothers and a sister." She didn't mention her sister wasn't with them anymore.

"Nerd or jock?" He threw back at her with a smirk.

She found herself smiling, forgiving him for being closed off. "Both I suppose. Swim team and Valedictorian."

"So, a control freak *and* overachiever."

A laugh escaped her throat as she shook her head. "You make it sound like a bad thing."

The flat road stretched out beneath the full moon, and a few headlights zipped by now and then. It was enough light that when she turned her head, she caught him studying her scar.

"And what made you choose law enforcement?" he asked.

She was surprised he didn't ask about the scar outright. "Now that," she sighed, "is a longer conversation for a day when I have the energy and courage to talk about it."

"It's a date then."

She glanced over at him, trying to figure out if he was serious. She couldn't tell. "Is it now?"

He picked up his Styrofoam cup and winked at her. "I have many questions, so it'll probably be a long date."

"Well, that sounds more like an interrogation than a date."

"Call it whatever you'd like. I know you control freaks like to label things, put them in their proper boxes."

A small puff of laughter escaped her lips.

"Also, an interrogation sounds fun, we could role-play."

She almost choked on the cold coffee she'd just put to her lips.

He laughed then. The first genuine laugh she'd heard from him. "Are you awake now?"

"I... yeah. Thanks, I guess." She glanced down at his left hand. No ring. That didn't mean there was no girlfriend in the picture. She cleared her throat. "What about you? What made you choose law enforcement?"

He blew out a breath, his hand fisting into a ball again. "I couldn't protect someone important to me. I suppose it's penance. Like maybe if I can protect someone else, I'll get closer to being forgiven."

The pain in his voice made her want to reach out and grab his hand, comfort him somehow. Softly she asked, "Forgiven by whom?"

After a few beats of silence, he whispered, "Myself."

Her brow quirked up. Maybe that's where all the guilt was coming from, not just the Amelia Larson case. His own personal sin that he couldn't forgive himself for.

After that confession, the silence between them was comfortable, but she was still keenly aware of his presence. Before she could be honest with herself about why she'd asked him along tonight, he broke the silence. "Will you let me know if anything comes of talking to Forester in the morning?"

"Sure," she agreed, forcing her tired brain back onto the case. Forester. That was going to be an interesting conversation.

ELEVEN

After three hours of sleep, Mila threw the covers back and dragged herself into a cold shower. Then sneaking a kiss on her sleeping daughter's cheek and giving a scratch to Oscar, she headed downstairs.

In the kitchen, Kittie sat at the table in her bathrobe with Houseplant Magazine and a steaming cup of coffee. "Good morning," she said softly as Mila descended the stairs. "Have a leftover pot pie warming in the oven for you. Coffee is fresh."

"Mmm. Thanks." Mila leaned over, giving Kittie's shoulders a one-arm hug. Kittie's hair wasn't braided for the day yet, so the damp, silver curtain hung down her back. Her rose-scented shampoo filled Mila's nose. "You're the best."

As Mila poured herself a cup of coffee, Kittie asked. "How's the search for little Conly Parks going?"

Mila added some cream from the fridge and shook her head. "Honestly, not well. I'm going to talk to one of the prime suspects this morning, but it would be so much easier to take a team in there and tear his place apart instead."

Kittie chuckled. "Yeah, those pesky privacy laws."

Mila smiled grimly as she pulled the golden-crusted chicken pie out of the oven and plated it. When she sat down across from Kittie, she sighed and stabbed it with a fork, watching the steam and creamy liquid spill out. "How's Harper's mode been these past few days?" She knew Paul had told Kittie about the drawing Harper had made at school. They'd asked her to keep an eye on how Harper was coping.

"She seems fine. She was really upset about Oscar getting sick. Oh, I have something to show you." She rose from the table and slipped outside through the sliding glass door. When she returned, she was holding an open baggie. "I followed Oscar around the yard last night to make sure he didn't get into anything. He was sniffing this. It was lying by the fence slats knocked over by the hurricane. I made sure he didn't eat it."

Taking the baggie from her, Mila held it up, frowning. There were two half-pieces of raw hotdog inside. *What the hell?* A cold chill ran under her skin. This was deliberate. Was this what Oscar had eaten when he'd gotten sick?

She stood and took the baggie over to the kitchen counter, grabbing a knife. When she sliced through the hot dog, the knife hit something hard. Digging the brown pellet out, she knew instantly what it was.

Rat poison.

Her heartbeat ticking up, she dug into both pieces of meat and pulled out a total of seven pellets. Anger and disbelief flooded through her as she processed what this meant.

"Someone poisoned Oscar and tried to do it a second time. Why?" Their neighbors loved Oscar. They'd never had any complaints about him. Why would someone do this?

She placed everything back in the baggie, then washed her hands and sat back down at the table, her mind reeling.

Kittie's complexion had gone white, her pale blue eyes watery with concern. "Who would do this?"

"I don't know. But make sure he only goes out on a leash for the time being." Mila checked her watch. She needed to get going.

Quickly taking a few bites of the pie to quiet her burning stomach, she wrapped up the rest and put it in the fridge.

Giving Kittie's shoulder a last squeeze of reassurance, she said, "Also make sure the doors are locked at all times. Especially this back door." They had a habit of leaving the sliding glass door unlocked, but with the downed fence piece, anyone could waltz into their backyard. And apparently, someone had.

Mila pulled through the gate of the Forester mansion and parked between the fountain and the front entrance.

Keep it friendly. Don't give anything away.

As she exited the SUV, she stopped. The garage bay doors were open. Not being able to pass up an opportunity to take a peek, she strolled over. It was a six-car garage. Her brows raised in appreciation as she took inventory of the millions of dollars staring back at her. A black Lambo, a white Mercedes-Benz E-class convertible, a black Ford F-150, a cream and gold Rolls-Royce Phantom, and a midnight blue classic Harley.

Who said money couldn't buy happiness?

The maid left her standing in the foyer while she went to fetch Roman, so Mila walked over to the wall-to-ceiling windows. Beyond the yard and pool, the Bay waters were calm and glistening under the morning sun. Rattlesnake Island was clearly visible a few miles away, a small bit of land with a flock of white birds circling it.

When she turned her head to the left, she stiffened. There was movement on Roman's yacht. Her eyes narrowed. Six men, that she could see, milling around with equipment. They were cleaning it.

Now why would that be?

She glanced back at Rattlesnake Island.

"Detective." Roman's voice echoed in the great room. She turned to face him. This time Roman seemed more closed off. He didn't take her to the backyard and get philosophical. He kept her there, standing in the cold marble entranceway. His arms were crossed, gray eyes shuttered, even as the harsh morning light revealed the small bloodshot veins running through them.

Mila clocked the defensive posture and then said, "I assume you know why I'm here."

"To accuse me of having something to do with a little girl's disappearance. Again." Despite his gaze hardening, the corner of his mouth ticked upward in amusement. "I'll save you the trouble. I've been home painting all day and night."

"And you of course have witnesses that can corroborate that?"

"Of course."

Mila didn't believe for one second that his staff couldn't be persuaded to lie with a bonus on their paycheck. She needed to change tactics. She lifted her hands with a smile. "Honestly, Roman, I'm a pretty good judge of character, and I don't think you had anything to do with either girl's disappearance. But my captain wants all bases covered and since you did paint Amelia and offered to paint Coco, that's what I'm doing."

His brows pressed down. "I offered to paint this little girl, Coco?"

"That's what her mother said." Mila pulled up a photo of Coco on her phone and held it out to him.

He studied it silently and then shrugged. "I don't remember her, but she does have that certain spark of joy and freedom in her eyes that would catch my attention."

Mila's gaze narrowed. "You don't remember her?"

"That's what I said." His jaw twitched. Anger. *Interesting*.

She cocked her head and studied him. "Do you think that's why they were targeted and taken? Did someone else see that spark in them?"

His eyes clouded with a different emotion mixed with the anger. "You'd have to ask the monsters who took them, Detective."

"You think it's two separate monsters?"

His brows shot up. "You don't?"

Did she?

She had no evidence that the two abductions were connected. Just a growing gut feeling. Also, the fact that Coco disappeared right after Amelia was found. But she would not believe it was the same perp until there was solid evidence. "I don't have an opinion one way or the other yet. I'm sure I will soon though." She smiled. "I noticed you're having your yacht detailed."

He glanced out the window. "Looks that way. I don't schedule cleaning and maintenance of the property. You'll have to speak with Ms. Vanore if you'd like information on that."

Mila raised a brow. "Is she here?"

"She is."

"Well, then if I could just have a word with her, I'll leave you to get back to your painting." She paused a beat and then said, "Oh wait, one more thing." She opened her phone, where she already had the IG post of Coco with his comment pulled up. She held it out in front of him. "You said you don't remember her, but you also follow Coco on social media."

His eyes narrowed as he read over his comment and then met hers. "Yes. I know it may make me seem like a creep, but as I've explained, I get my inspiration from young girls, so I do follow many on social media."

She turned the phone toward herself and read his comment. "Fierce innocence frozen in time. If only it were that simple." Her gaze flicked up to hold his. "With a crown emoji."

One shoulder jerked up as he crossed his arms defensively. "All women are born queens. The world just makes them forget that fact."

Mila nodded, thinking about his Marylin Monroe painting. He was consistent with his explanations, but was that just a carefully crafted cover to be able to stalk little girls? "You know how else you can freeze a little girl in time? By making sure she doesn't grow up."

A corner of his mouth ticked up. "Yes, I suppose you're right. Very clever, Detective. I'll go fetch Ms. Vanore for you now. Good day."

⁂

Mila drove back to the station. Ms. Vanore had shown her the digital spreadsheet where the yacht cleaning was on the schedule. She said it was a bi-yearly event scheduled at the beginning of each year. They could always subpoena her bank records and see if there were any extra payments recently in exchange for her silence. But right now, they didn't have enough to convince a judge.

As she drove, she found herself searching every parking lot, scanning inside every car she passed. *Where are you, Coco?* It was terrifying how easily a child could disappear. Even in a town as small as Edgewater.

⁂

When she arrived back at the station, the parking lot was crowded with press vans. Reporters were grouped around the front doors with shoulder video cameras and fuzzy microphones, a buzz of conversation in the air.

Captain Bartol and Mayor Sheila Starek were standing in front of the doors, hunched over a piece of paper. When the mayor squeezed Captain Bartol's arm and nodded, the two women moved closer to the crowd, and the captain cleared her throat.

"Good afternoon, my name is Captain Bartol, Edgewater PD. Today I'm here to provide an update on the search for six-year-old Conly Parks. As you know, she was taken from Garden Park Elementary playground around five PM yesterday."

She went on to describe Coco and what she was wearing when she was abducted. "I'm also joined by Mayor Starek." Shiela nodded at the crowd. "We have called in the CART team and have the assistance of law enforcement from five counties. These investigators are following active leads, and evidence gathered along with tips from the public. We ask businesses with surveillance cameras facing West Pine Road to turn in any video you have from last night to our precinct." She checked her notes. "Also, we do have an image of the abductor, which we will be releasing to the public shortly. There's an eight-hundred number set up for anyone who feels they have information to contribute." She paused as a wave of excited murmurs rolled through the crowd.

Mila spotted Elly Prescott in the front, her Suncoast Times cameraman by her side. A surge of something dark and prickly ran through her veins, heating her face. With effort, she forced herself to move her attention back to Captain Bartol. She was having a hard time processing the words over the images her mind was conjuring up of Prescott and Paul together.

She pulled out her phone and fired off a text to Detective Scott before she could question her own motivations: *Talked to Forester. Tell you about it over dinner tonight?*

His answer came immediately: *Just tell me when and where*

Inside the precinct was even more chaotic than last night. Most of the activity centered around the conference room, but there were unfamiliar faces in the bullpen, too. The heightened energy and noise had Mila's nerves on edge.

Frank sat at his desk, the phone pressed to his ear. Aiden stood in the hallway talking to one of the Clearwater detectives. She made her way back to the relative quiet of Matt's office. His door was open, and he was leaning into the computer screen, watching something intently.

She knocked on the door frame and then entered when he flicked his tired gaze to her in acknowledgment. Walking behind him to have a peek at his screen, she asked, "Street footage from around Weeden Park?"

"Yeah." He sighed and rubbed the black stubble on his square jaw. "Patrol rounded up half a dozen surveillance videos so far. I don't even know what I'm looking for." He motioned to the steno pad beside his elbow. "Just writing down every make and model of car that drove down Pine and Grove within the hour after the abduction."

Mila scanned the long list as she asked, "Did you get Coco's IG information sent to—"

Her breath hitched and got caught in her chest. She fell forward and held her finger on the steno pad. "Rolls Royce? Can you pull that footage up?"

Matt's back straightened as he caught her energy. "Sure." He checked the time stamp note beside it and pulled up the video. "Here you go."

Mila watched the cream and gold Rolls Royce crawl down Grove Street. "How many of these do you think there are in town?"

He scoffed. "One. You know who owns it?"

Her pulse was racing as she smiled at Matt. "I do. Our now number one suspect. Forester."

"Huh." Matt hit print on his keyboard.

"We'll need to expand our request for surveillance video, see if we can figure out where that car went. If he was the abductor and didn't go back to his house, he could've stashed her somewhere else."

"On it," Matt said.

Mila took the printout of the Rolls Royce to Captain Bartol as soon as the press conference ended and explained how she'd seen the car in Forester's garage this morning. "He told me he was at home. Matt's working on getting additional surveillance to see where the car went from there. Do you think it's enough to get a search warrant? Between this and the Instagram post?"

Captain Bartol chewed the inside of her lip as she studied the printout. "We can't assume Forester was the one driving the car. Maybe someone else in the household has access to it." She shook her head as she finally lifted her gaze. "If it were anyone else, I'd say let's give it a shot. But that family has too much political pull in this town. When we take our run at him, it's got to be bulletproof." Her eyes hardened. "We need more."

Mila nodded, even as her shoulders fell. "We'll get it. Permission for surveillance of Forester?"

"No room in our budget, but I'll see if the sheriff's department can take some shifts."

Aiden was back at his desk, and Frank was off the phone. Mila motioned them over. When she had both of their attention, she dropped the printout on Aiden's desk. "This is Forester's Rolls. It's headed south on Grove Street twenty-five minutes after the abduction. He lied to me this morning and told me he was home painting all day."

Frank's arms were crossed as he stared at the printout silently. "If in fact, it was him driving."

Aiden scoffed. "Would you let anyone else drive your Rolls?" He turned to Mila. "No one lives in that house besides the help and the mother, right?"

Mila nodded. "As far as I know."

Aiden's whiskey-colored eyes brightened with anticipation. "What did Cap say?"

Mila shook her head. "We don't have enough for a search warrant. We need to get something more solid."

While she had them both there, she also filled them in on her conversation with Garrett Levington last night, leaving out the fact that Detective Scott had been with her. Another thing she wouldn't allow herself to think too much about.

"And you believe Levington?" Frank asked when she told them about the Christmas ham comment being about his boat getting repoed.

Mila rubbed at a knot in her lower back. "Not before we check out his story."

"I'm on it," Frank said. "Maybe we can stop wasting our time on the asshole."

They watched Frank stroll purposefully back to his desk.

"Anything come from any of the interviews?" Mila asked Aiden.

Aiden's lips tightened in frustration as he leaned back in his chair. "Not anything helpful yet."

She nodded a greeting at the CART commander as he passed them. "Nothing that would suggest this case is related to Amelia Larson?"

"No, but if it were... that may be good news. If it's the same guy, maybe he'll keep her alive for a while, like he did Amelia. Either way, the sheriff's department went out this morning to check Rattlesnake Island in case..." He shot her a grim look. He didn't have to finish the sentence. She knew what they were looking for out there. "Captain Bartol also asked waste management not to collect in the area around the park until we've searched all the dumpsters."

Mila squeezed her eyes shut for a moment. Standard procedure but still... unthinkable. "All right. Where is our priority? How do we get more on Forester?"

There were so many balls up in the air right now, so many paths they needed to investigate, her exhausted brain was starting to lose the plot.

"The CART volunteers are going door to door in every neighborhood where Coco knew someone and every neighborhood surrounding the school. Eyewitness accounts are our best shot at any information right now. As far as Forester... I honestly don't know what we can do."

Mila thought about the CART volunteers. "I'm sure they're being very thorough but unfortunately, I think the biggest risk factor here is Coco's Instagram account. Besides Forester following her, someone found her once through that account. According to that someone, Coco's photos have information that gives away her location."

"If someone else found her through social media, then there's no connection to our town." Aiden scrubbed a rough hand over his five o'clock shadow. "No evidence here to be found. It's up to the FBI."

"And that would also mean her case and Amelia's aren't connected. Amelia didn't have social media." She fought the helplessness trying to worm its way in. She wouldn't accept it.

Aiden folded his arms and stared at her. "I hear a *but*."

She shook her head like she was trying to clear it. "But I feel this almost invisible thread between them."

Aiden sighed and plucked a baggie from his desk, offered her some of the homemade granola. She declined. "It does seem like a big coincidence that right after Amelia's body was dumped, Coco was taken."

"Yeah, and they were both six years old, and we don't believe in coincidences." Just then Mila's phone vibrated. She didn't recognize the number. "Detective Harlow."

"Detective, this is Roman Forester. Do you have a moment?"

Mila froze and mouthed "Forester" to Aiden. "Sure. What can I do for you?"

"I've just watched the videos of Coco's abduction."

"Watched the videos? How?" she demanded. They had released a still photo to the press, but not either of the videos. Someone had sent them to him. Someone from the department.

"That's of no consequence. What is though is I can see why you came to me. The curly hair, the limp. It appears someone is trying to frame me."

Mila held Aiden's stare, but her mind was busy grabbing at scenarios and tossing them aside. "Why would someone do that?" she asked skeptically.

"Most likely to throw the heat my way instead of theirs," he said slowly, like he was explaining something to a child.

Mila didn't appreciate the condescension. "Do you have anyone in mind?"

"I'm an artist, not a mob boss. I haven't made many enemies in my life."

"That you know of," Mila quipped. When he stayed silent, she said. "All right. If you can think of anyone, make me a list and I'll check them out. Meanwhile..." she saw Aiden's mouth quirk up in a smirk. He knew where she would go next. "Can you tell me why your one-of-a-kind Rolls Royce was spotted driving away from the park around the time Coco was abducted?"

She waited. She would have preferred to ask him in person to see his reaction, but she knew this was her only shot. She couldn't harass the man and go to his house again. The silence dragged on, and she let it.

Finally, Forester sighed. "I'm sorry I lied to you, Detective. But... my alibi is very... personal, and I'm afraid a bit embarrassing."

"Would you rather suffer a bit of embarrassment or an arrest for impeding an investigation?"

"Well, when you put it that way." He chuckled. "All right. I'd appreciate it if you could make sure this doesn't get leaked to the press."

"Leaks are by definition not in my control, but I can promise I will not share this information with anyone unnecessarily." She wanted to add "as you well know" since someone obviously leaked the abduction videos to him, but she decided not to antagonize him.

"Fair enough. Are you familiar with Club Bombshell in Clearwater?"

"I'm not."

"Not surprised. It's sort of an underground club… a sex club for those of us who don't fit into society's norms." He didn't elaborate but he didn't have to. "I assume you're not going to just take my word for it, so Miss Scarlett Aberdene will be waiting for you any time after five tonight. She'll provide you with proof I was there."

Mila blinked and kept her voice neutral as she said, "We'll be in touch" and then hung up. She turned to Aiden; brows raised. "Looks like I'm going to a sex club tonight for Mr. Forester's alibi."

Aiden held up his hands, amusement pinching the corners of his mouth. "Sorry, I'd offer to go with you, but I prefer not sleeping on the couch."

Mila waved him off. "Don't worry. I have to talk to Detective Scott tonight anyway. I'll make him go with me."

"Detective Scott, huh?" Aiden leaned back in his chair, fighting a grin. "He's single?"

She narrowed her eyes at him. "And going to stay that way." She picked up the printout of the Rolls Royce, intending to take it back to her own desk. Before she did, she felt the need to remind Aiden or defend herself. "You know he was the lead on Amelia's case, if anyone can spot a link between these two cases, it would be him."

"Just saying." Aiden's deep-set brown eyes danced with humor. "This job can't be your whole life."

She straightened her shoulders and tucked her frustration away. "It's not." Then she went back to her own desk with his grunts of disagreement following her.

It's not, she insisted to herself. She had Harper. And other family.

And Paul had Elly Prescott.

Her mood souring, she collapsed into her chair and logged into the computer to check her emails. One from Zansi caught her eye. It was Amelia's final autopsy report. She skimmed it, getting the gist.

No cause of death could be determined, but there was also no sexual assault. She breathed out in relief. So, why keep the little girl alive for three years? She had to figure out his motivation. It would be the key to finding him.

She called Detective Scott, and he picked up on the second ring. "Scott."

"Hey, it's Mila. I just got a final report for Amelia's autopsy. No cause of death could be determined, and she wasn't sexually assaulted. Thought you'd want to know."

There was some rustling paper noise and then he cleared his throat. "That's good news. Yeah, thanks for letting me know."

She squeezed her eyes shut and continued, "I also need to ask you a favor. Do you want to go to Club Bombshell in Clearwater with me tonight to check out Mr. Forester's alibi? It's a um...sex club." The silence was deafening. "I would prefer not to go alone. I'm not sure what I'm walking into. Be great to have backup." She should shut up now before her face caught on fire.

A low chuckle vibrated through the receiver. "You can pick me up from the station since it's on the way. I should be done here around six."

"Great. See you then." She quickly hung up and dropped her head into her hands.

Jesus, Mila. Stop acting like a middle schooler.

She went back to checking her emails. After that, she pulled up Google and added some keywords to start her search: "Six-year-old girl" "birthday" "abducted"

Then she scrolled through the results:

Six-year-old fights off abductor in Miami by biting him, Ring doorbell camera captures abduction attempt in Ohio by a serial abductor, six-year-old vanished with her mother in Illinois, six-year-old in Texas falls out of tree, dies on her birthday, three-year-old abducted from birthday party in Tampa, found suffocated two weeks later.

Mila's stomach roiled and clenched in anger. She pushed away from the desk. She couldn't read anymore right now. Instead, she gathered her things and headed outside.

On the way to pick up Detective Scott, Mila stopped by and checked on Raelynn. They'd put barriers up around her yard and a smattering of press was camped out in the road.

An unfamiliar female officer stepped out of her patrol car when Mila approached with a friendly wave.

The officer eyed Mila's badge and then said, "They took Ms. Parks away in an ambulance about an hour ago. Couldn't get her to calm down." She shook her head. "Can't say I wouldn't need to be sedated, too, if it was my baby. Any leads yet?"

"A few," was all Mila could say. She dug out a card. "Can you let me know when she gets back home?"

"Sure thing, Detective. Good luck out there."

Mila nodded, but she didn't need luck. She needed to keep digging and maybe just catch a small goddamn break.

TWELVE

Detective Scott had apparently received her text that she was on her way. He was standing in front of Crystal Harbor PD, talking on his phone when she pulled up. He waved, ended his call and then lifted himself into the passenger seat.

His dark eyes glistened with mischief. "I would've suggested dinner as our first date, but hey, whatever floats your boat."

She groaned and then laughed as she pressed the gas pedal and steered them toward what was sure to be an awkward-as-hell meeting.

As they drove deeper into the underbelly of Tampa, glittering city lights and shiny glass buildings were replaced with gritty streets, filled with dirty puddles of rainwater and graffiti-covered warehouses. The club address was a square concrete building that had been painted black with a red door.

"This it?" Detective Scott asked.

"Yep." Mila eyed the area, staying alert as they parked and made their way to the front door.

There was a keycode lock and there were no windows.

Mila knocked. No response. She glanced up and spotted the camera pointing at the door. She plucked her gold shield from her belt and held it up. The door clicked and Detective Scott pulled it open. "After you."

The squat hallway was dark, lit only with a single purple bulb. A large tattooed, pierced bouncer in a black leather vest stood just inside, glowering at them.

"Detective Mila Harlow," she said. "Scarlett Aberdene is expecting us."

He ran his gaze over them both as he growled into a walkie-talkie. "This way," he grunted in obvious irritation.

Guess they don't get many cops in here.

They followed him to the end of the hallway. On the left was a woman in a windowed counter, watching them suspiciously. The bodyguard nodded at her. With an eye-roll and a smack of her gum, she buzzed open the door.

They stepped inside and Mila's nervous system kicked into high gear. Her fingertips moved to rest near her weapon. The music was so loud, it vibrated her bones. Strobe lights made it impossible to see anything as solid in the large space. The perfect atmosphere to forget about the outside world, release inhibitions and give in to whatever fantasy your heart desires.

Being a card-carrying control freak member, Mila couldn't see the appeal.

Logan pressed closer to her, his arm brushing her shoulder. This would also be a perfect place for an ambush. She kept her eyes locked on the strobing figure they were following.

Through a dense, sweet-scented fog, she caught glimpses of people, bodies writhing together on a dance floor in one undulating mass, and bodies sprawled out on large sofas around the edges. The chaos prickled her skin. Sweat formed around her hairline and her armpits.

Logan's warm palm pressed against her lower back as he kept her close. She hated the comfort she was getting from his touch, his presence beside her. It made her feel weak.

Luckily, the next room they were led through was less chaotic. Instead of strobes, the room was lit with a steady purple lighting.

Logan dropped his hand, leaving a cold spot on her back.

The fog still hung heavy in the air, but a stage was visible. On that stage was a man clad in a speedo, bikini top, heels, a long blonde wig, and covered in fluorescent green paint, showing off his dance skills. Some kind of techno dance music screeched over the speakers.

More people sat at round tables, drinking and enjoying the show, some in elaborate costumes and wigs, or black leather outfits and some in barely anything. A large bar outlined in pink neon lights curved around the entire wall to their right.

They passed through that room into a hallway with doors on each side. Mila and Logan shared a glance, and she knew they were on the same page. They had a murder and abduction to worry about, whatever was going on behind those doors wasn't their concern.

They finally reached the end of the hall, and the bouncer rapped his knuckles on the door then opened it. A tall trans woman rose from her desk and sashayed toward them. She had sleek black hair, arms like a bodybuilder, and a tight, red-lipped smile.

She held out a hand adorned with red nails and thick, gold jewelry. "Hello, detectives. You can call me Scarlett." She waved them forward to follow her deeper into the space. "Normally, I wouldn't invade a patron's privacy and share this information without a court order, but Mr. Forester has requested it, so I've agreed." She walked them over to a wall of monitors on their right. "You can watch here." Then she left them and went to the computer on her desk.

Logan folded his arms, scanning the different feeds on each screen which currently monitored the club.

Mila watched the woman at the desk as she clicked away on her keyboard. Scarlett was confident and didn't seem to be hiding anything or harboring any sort of grudge toward them. This was just business for her.

Finally, Scarlett pointed to the wall in front of them. "I'll bring it up on the top left monitor. The day in question, Mr. Forester arrived around six PM." They watched as the front door camera captured Mr. Forester walking in with a duffel bag. "He went straight to the Queen room, which is where our performers put on their costumes, hair and makeup." They watched him enter a side door behind the stage. "Of course, there are no cameras in there for privacy reasons." She fast-forwarded the video. "And then you see him come out an hour later."

The video played without sound. "Where?" Mila asked, squinting at the monitor.

Scarlett rewound the video and paused it on a woman in a long red wig and chainmail dress. "There." After a few moments, she let the video play.

Mila studied it. If it wasn't for the limp in his step, she wouldn't have recognized him. In fact, could she even say it was him? The video camera was pointing down and captured the whole room, so not very good quality.

"Can you show us his movements after that please?" Mila instructed.

Scarlett nodded patiently. "After that, he went to the bar and got a drink. Talked to some of the other patrons for a while. Then took the stage for his act."

They watched his act silently, there was no sound, but he held a microphone and sang. Scarlett fast-forwarded the video through the act. It was forty minutes long. He bowed as the people around the stage rose and gave him a standing ovation, and then he disappeared back into the Queen room at 7:25 PM.

"Is there an exit in the Queen room that leads outside?" Mila asked.

"No."

She studied the woman's face. "Mind if I check on the way out?"

"Of course not." Scarlett smiled pleasantly and returned to her seat behind the desk.

So, is this what he's hiding? Why she has the feeling he doesn't show his true self to the outside world?

Mila walked over and dropped a card on Scarlett's desk. "I'll need you to send a copy of that surveillance video to me. Thanks for your time."

She and Logan stepped out of the office. As they moved back down the hallway, one of the doors opened and a couple emerged, still clinging to one another. They were laughing, the tall man pinning the other against the wall and taking his mouth in a brutal kiss.

"Excuse us," Mila said as they squeezed by.

The two men barely glanced at them, too caught up in the lust that was glowing in their eyes, animating their hands to clutch at each other.

Mila thought about the first time she and Paul let their mutual attraction loose. It was just like that, all lips and hands and fiery lust. That was so long ago, and it had been so long since she'd felt that kind of desire, she wasn't sure she was even capable of it anymore. Was her passion lying dormant? Or truly dead?

They checked the Queen room, which held two rows of tables with lighted mirrors, racks of elaborate clothing, and a few startled patrons getting ready at the tables, but no exit.

By the time they stepped back out into the muggy night air, a frisson of irritation buzzed around her brain.

"What do you think?" Logan asked as they walked back to her SUV.

She didn't know Logan very well, but his tone dripped with the same doubt she was feeling. They stopped in front of her vehicle, and Mila stared back at the building.

She was too aware of his solid presence in front of her, the unbridled intimacy they'd just glimpsed throwing her off balance. She took a step back. She was a detective right now, not a woman, she reminded herself.

"I don't know why he'd send us here if it wasn't him. That'd be too risky. But... I also don't know, with the costume, makeup and wig," she shook her head, "it could be someone else and we'd never know. There was the limp, but someone could fake that if they were helping him with an alibi."

Logan's gaze fell to her mouth and then raised to her eyes. "Yeah, I believe that was him walking through the door and entering the Queen room. But after that? Did he stay?" He questioned.

Mila cocked her head. "Or did he go back out to his car, where he had little Coco stashed and drive her somewhere else, alibi established?" She forced herself to take another step away from him. "Come on, I'll get you home."

She navigated the streets of downtown Tampa, inching forward at a traffic light. Her mind rehashed everything they'd learned so far. "Going back to the Amelia Larson case for a moment... I'm grateful that she wasn't sexually assaulted, but that leaves two big questions. Why did her abductor keep her alive for three years? And then why kill her now?" She glanced over at Logan, who was staring out the passenger window, watching people walk down the sidewalk. "Any theories?"

His voice was tight with sorrow as he whispered, "People can justify anything to themselves, darlin'."

Mila ignored the rush of heat to her face at his softened tone and pet name. She gripped the steering wheel tighter. "Let's say these two cases are connected," she said slowly, her mind trying to form the connection. "Same person, two six-year-old girls who the perp didn't abduct to assault. Why take them then? I guess if Forester is the abductor, that would make sense as to why Amelia wasn't sexually assaulted. That's obviously not his kink. But he does have a weird obsession with little girls."

A few miles down the road, Logan sighed. His head fell back against the seat. "Maybe it wasn't about taking the girls at all but getting them away from their current situation."

She changed lanes to get on the highway. The sky lit up with heat lighting in the distance. "What do you mean?"

He turned to her then, his gaze more like an assessment, like he was trying to figure out if he could really trust her. Finally, he nodded to himself. "You asked me if I had a theory. Amelia Larson was shot by her drunk mother's boyfriend, not exactly a safe home life. And Coco's mother was exploiting her to adult men online for money. Even after the danger became real when one of those men showed up at her house, the mother put money over her child's safety and refused to take down the Instagram account."

"True." Mila felt this new angle expand her way of thinking about both investigations. "But that would mean the abductor knew both girls personally, knew that they were in a less-than-ideal living condition. But they lived in separate towns and went to separate schools." She drummed her fingers on the steering wheel. "I guess we need to start comparing friend and acquaintance groups of both girls, see if we can find an overlap. I'll have to go back through Amelia's case files and make a list."

"I can help with that," Logan said, his voice a low rumble. "If you'd like. We could start tonight. I'll grab my truck; you grab the files and meet me back at my house." At her hesitation, he added, "Unless you have another lead you need to track down tonight?"

That wasn't why she was hesitating. Could she trust herself to be alone with this man and not get sidetracked? Probably not, but his help was welcomed. "No, this seems like the best path forward right now."

By the time Mila updated the team, asked Matt to go through the festival videos to see if there were any signs of Forester when Amelia was taken, loaded Amelia's file boxes into her SUV, and made the drive to Logan's house, it was almost nine at night. The area was nothing but shadows. No streetlights, no neighboring porch lights.

She sat in his driveway next to his pickup for a minute, as the automatic light above the garage door flicked on, and video-called Harper to say goodnight.

Harper seemed unusually quiet, and Mila hoped she was just tired from her day, but she promised herself she would find an hour to spend with her daughter tomorrow. Maybe take her for ice cream.

Mila started pulling the boxes from the backseat when Logan stepped out. He greeted her and then carried three of them into the house, leaving her to carry one as she followed him inside.

He dropped them on the floor next to a brown leather sofa. His hair was damp, and he smelled like soap. He'd also changed into jeans and a white T-shirt.

Mila glanced around. The place was tidy with minimal furniture. A generic painting of a cow hung above a gas fireplace. Nothing personal, not one family photo in the room. Country music played softly from a stereo system set up in the corner of the room. On the glass coffee table sat boxes of Chinese food.

Her stomach clenched at the scent.

"Hope you like Chinese." Logan motioned for her to take a seat.

"I do, thanks. Though at this point I would probably eat your couch."

With a chuckle, he lowered himself next to her and dished the food onto two plates. She accepted the plate, scooted back against the couch and turned her body toward him as she speared a piece of chicken. "How long have you lived here?"

"Fifteen years." He took a bite and then let himself see the house through her eyes. "Guess I could've put more effort into decorating," he said sheepishly. "I spend more time at the station than here, though. I'm sure you know how it is." He chewed thoughtfully as he stared at her. "How do you do it with a daughter? Not feel guilty for being gone so much?"

"That's the million-dollar question, isn't it." She sighed. "Honestly, I just live with the guilt." She poked at a piece of broccoli. "Paul's mom lives with us, takes care of Harper. She's an absolute saint, and I wouldn't be able to do this job without her." Mila swallowed a bite of rice and chicken and reached for one of the water bottles next to the food boxes.

They ate in comfortable silence for a few minutes.

"So, you were going to tell me how you got that scar."

Mila glanced up from her plate. Logan's dark eyes held hers with curiosity. "I'll tell you what," she smirked, "if we get through all four boxes tonight, I'll tell you the story."

An unknown emotion softened Logan's gaze. "I do enjoy a challenge. You got yourself a deal."

When they'd finished, Mila helped carry their plates and the leftovers into the kitchen. While she rinsed the plates and put them in the dishwasher, he pulled a bottle of scotch and two glasses from the top cabinet.

At Mila's raised brow, he smirked. "Not trying to get you drunk, promise." He winked, "Not tonight anyway."

"Detective Scott, are you flirting with me?" she chided playfully.

"Goddamn, if you have to ask, I'm not doing it right." He grinned and motioned for her to follow. When they sat back on the leather sofa, he poured two fingers of the bourbon into each tumbler and handed her one. "To Coco's safety." He clinked her glass.

"And a quick solve." Mila took a mouthful of the honey-brown liquor in her mouth and let it slide down her throat, burning a path into her stomach. It warmed her from the inside out, and she felt her shoulders relax for the first time all day. She cocked her head. "So, you're a bourbon guy? I feel like I don't know you at all."

A slow smile spread on his face. "Now who's flirting, detective?"

The heat in her belly moved to her core as his eyes dropped to her lips. "You're right." She reluctantly turned away. "We need to focus." Setting her glass on the coffee table, she rose and grabbed the top box. Then she dropped it by his feet with a grin. "Don't say I never gave you anything." Lifting the second box, she dropped it on the floor by her own feet and pulled out her leather notebook and a pen.

Logan reached for his notebook with a groan. "You know what they say about all work and no play, right?"

"*They* don't have a little girl to find."

"Touché."

They worked side by side, going through every note and file to write down any names mentioned while the music played in the background, filling the silence.

Witnesses, friends, acquaintances, neighbors, teachers, school employees, anyone that had any kind of contact with Amelia Larson. It was almost 11:30 by the time Logan threw down his pen and tossed back the last of his Scotch. "Done."

Mila leaned forward, glanced at his list and groaned. "There must be over two hundred names there." She held up her own pad. "On mine, too."

She finished going through the last notes in her box, adding another twenty people to the list.

Logan had wandered off into the back of the house. She stood, stretched her back and then went to the kitchen for more water. Logan returned as she leaned against the kitchen counter, lost in thought with the glass in her hand.

She blinked, coming back to the present as he stood in front of her. Her chin tilted up to meet his eyes. A spark flickered there, like a flame trying to come back to life. He stepped forward, running a long finger from her jaw, down her neck, tracing her scar. "You were going to tell me about this. A deal is a deal."

A shiver rolled through her body at the gravel in his voice. She had to stop herself from just stepping into him and getting lost in something physical instead of rehashing the past.

When he noticed her hesitation, he held her stare and his voice was a whisper. "It's okay if you don't want to. Some things shouldn't see the light of day again, even in words."

She bit her bottom lip. His eyes darkened. Even in the fluorescent kitchen light, they were absorbing light instead of reflecting it. "I've had enough therapy that I can talk about it, so it's fine. It was just so long ago."

His eyes flicked from hers down to her lips. He reached out and gently took the glass from her, setting it on the counter, then rested a hand on either side of her body, trapping her against the counter. His breath was warm against her mouth as he said, "Your choice. We don't have to talk at all."

Mila's heart thumped in her chest, but not from fear. From the need in those dark eyes, the hooded desire as he held himself back, giving her the opportunity to push him away. She didn't.

He pulled back one final time, gazing into her eyes before he leaned in, his warm lips pressing just below her ear, then moving down her jaw and neck, trailing her scar with soft kisses. She couldn't stop the moan that escaped her throat when his teeth grazed her collarbone. Well, that answered the question of whether her libido was dead or just dormant.

He breathed her in as he made his way back up her neck, running the tip of his nose up over her jaw, then capturing her mouth with his. He tasted like heat and bourbon. His hand moved to the back of her head, holding her so he could press into her harder.

She wasn't sure how long the kiss lasted or even what planet she was on when she finally pulled away. She wasn't even sure why she pulled away. She knew her face was flushed as she rested a hand on his chest, his breath as ragged as hers, and gave him an apologetic smile. "I should go."

He pressed his forehead against hers for a moment before taking a step back with a moan and reaching for her hand. She let herself enjoy the warmth and strength in his grip as he silently led her back out into the living room. When he released her, the broken connection left her cold. But she couldn't let herself get distracted. Finding Coco was the only thing that mattered right now.

They stared at the pile of files that needed to be boxed back up. He rubbed the back of his neck roughly. "You can come back for these tomorrow if you want. I'll pack 'em up before I leave in the morning."

"Thanks." She grabbed the two lists they had compiled off the table. "I'll round up some volunteers to go through the names and cross-reference them with Coco's list."

"Hey," he said, his tone rough with need and something darker. Sadness? Regret? "I'm here for *anything* you need. Just name it."

Her gaze caught on his, and she saw the promise there, the heat, the desire. Message received. Was she a coward for leaving? All signs pointed to yes.

THIRTEEN
Coco

Don't talk to strangers, Mommy had warned her. But she'd watched Mommy on her phone, talking to strangers for hours, texting and laughing. There must be times when it was okay. And he wasn't a stranger, not exactly. And he had a beautiful doll to give her. And not just one. He said there was a whole box of them she could have with clothes, shoes and everything. Her mom didn't tell her what to do in that case. But his eyes and smile seemed kind. He wouldn't hurt her. He wanted to give her a gift. That's what he had said, and why wouldn't she believe him? He had kept his promise. There was a whole box of dolls, with tiny heels, necklaces, princess crowns, gowns, jackets, purses. She had dressed them all up for the ball and had a big party. Now she was tired and wanted to go home. She wondered if the man told her mom where she was. She padded over to the door and pulled on it like she'd done a dozen times already. Still stuck. The room didn't have any windows to tell her if it was dark outside. She didn't even know if she'd been here two days or a week. There was a tiny fridge humming in the corner with juice boxes, water and some fruit. The juice box was blurry as she took it from the fridge, her tears making everything shimmer. She sniffed them back.

Big girls don't cry. Only babies did and she wasn't a baby.

Then she went to the mattress and sat crisscross applesauce. She picked up a blue crayon and the picture she'd started drawing earlier of her and Mommy at the beach. Her mom would love it. She'd give it to her soon, she just knew it. Right?

Her chest tightened, and she couldn't take a breath. Her hand pressed against her belly, against the sparkly blue dress he'd given her. Tears dropped onto the ocean she'd colored, darkening spots. Her gaze darted around the small space as she whimpered, "Mommy."

Fourteen

The media room was already crowded when Mila arrived at the station at seven AM. A group briefing would start soon. She settled in beside Aiden with her large coffee. Frank sat on his other side, cleaning his glasses with his tie. She leaned forward and addressed them both. "Anything new?"

Frank's face was pinched and pale as he shook his head. "Besides my soon-to-be ex trying to padlock my front door, no."

Mila and Aiden shared a sympathetic smile. "Sorry, Frank," she said. "That's bold."

"More like psychotic," he grunted, shoving his glasses back on.

"You do know how to pick 'em," Aiden said with a laugh.

"Can't argue with that," Frank answered with a shake of his head. "If pickin' crazy bitches was an Olympic sport, I'd be a fuckin' gold medalist."

Mila rolled her eyes but knew better than to take the bait. Luckily Captain Bartol and the CART team commander, who looked like a skinny Santa Claus, strolled in at that moment and stood in front of the room.

"All right," Captain started, then waited until the room grew silent. "We have a lot to cover, and no time to waste so let's get to it. Mr. Yarnell here is going to bring us up to speed on all the relevant information the CART volunteers have collected." She motioned to Aiden. "Then Detective Reyes, our witness coordinator, will give us a summary and hand out leads to follow up on." She glanced down at the notebook in her hand. "Frank." She scanned the crowd until she locked eyes with Frank. "You've been monitoring incoming leads, anything to give patrol to follow up on?"

He nodded. "A few credible things, yes."

"All right and Detective Harlow." Her gaze found Mila's. "You have some things to share with the others?"

"Yes."

"Okay then, that's the order we'll give out information. I'll start with some items. There has been no attempt by the kidnapper to contact Raelynn Parks for ransom. The local FBI office is investigating Coco's IG account and the individuals who follow the account. So far, they haven't come up with any solid suspects. Right now our main suspect is Mr. Roman Forester. Detective Harlow can speak more about that. Pinellas Sherriff's Department has agreed to help out with surveillance, but it won't be twenty-four-seven. We need more evidence for a search warrant for his property." She glanced over at Mr. Yarnell. "The floor is yours."

Mr. Yarnell filled them in on all the relevant information the CART Team had gathered, which took about thirty minutes. Mila jotted down some notes as he talked but nothing really stood out that got her excited.

When he was done, Aiden stood and delivered his notes.

Frank's turn was next, and he handed Sergeant Brown a folder of leads to pass out to patrol, explaining the important points.

When it was Mila's turn, she stood and explained Forester's alibi at the club and how the costume, along with the angle of the video, made it a weak alibi. Especially since his Rolls was spotted near Weeden Park after the abduction. And then she added, "Forester was also connected to the Amelia Larson case. She's the girl who was abducted three years ago, when she was six, and whose body just turned up last week on Rattlesnake Island which, coincidentally or not, is visible from his mansion. Forester also painted her portrait. If these two cases are connected, we need to be thorough with that line of investigation. It could give us our motive." She held up the two sheets of names. "I've worked with the lead detective on the Amelia Larson case to write down a list of all the people named in her investigation. I need volunteers to cross reference these names with the Coco Parks case and see if there's an individual involved in both."

Mr. Yarnell held up a hand. "Get copies of those lists to me, and I'll hand them out to our volunteers. I'm sure they can get through them in a few hours today."

She nodded. "Thank you."

"Is there any other evidence these two cases are connected?" Captain Bartol asked.

She sighed regretfully. "No."

※

Mila took a break around four PM to pick up Harper. They sat at an outdoor table at Harper's favorite ice cream shop, Oscar stretched out beneath their feet. Which reminded her, she still needed to tell Paul about his mom finding the hotdogs with rat poison in their yard.

"How was Krav Maga class?" Mila asked, licking the vanilla cone she'd ordered.

Harper shrugged and dipped her spoon into the layer of gummy worms she'd added to her rainbow sherbert. "Fine, I guess. The boys smell funny and laugh at me when I can't do the moves." Her blue eyes flicked up. "Why can't I just take like an art class or something?"

Because you can't defend yourself with a paintbrush.

"You can do that, too, if you'd like." Mila's lips pursed in frustration. How to explain to Harper she needed to be able to defend herself without instilling fear? Maybe she'd ask the child psychologist about this. Their appointment wasn't for another three weeks though. It was the soonest they could get

Harper in. "What if we practiced more at home? It's just muscle memory. The more you practice, the faster you'll get better."

"When? When can we practice?" Harper asked, her nose flaring with a burst of frustration or anger, which was completely unlike her. She was always such an easygoing child.

Mila caught a flash of her sister in that expression and her whole being felt heavy, weighed down with guilt. "Fair point, sunshine. I'm sorry I'm not home more. I'd much rather spend all my time with you, believe me. That's just not our life."

Harper's anger drained from her as quickly as it had risen. "I know." She shoved a spoonful of sherbert into her mouth. After she swallowed, she asked, "Do you think you'll find that other little girl alive? The one who got taken from her school?"

Mila stared at her daughter. They hadn't talked about Coco yet. Mila had hoped she hadn't heard about the little girl's abduction, but of course she had. This was a small town and big news traveled fast. Leaning down, she offered Oscar the end of her cone, which he took gently from her fingers. Then she wiped her hands with a napkin and laced her fingers on the table. "We are doing everything possible to bring her home alive, Harper. There are hundreds of people searching for her. I have hope that we'll find her soon."

Harper stared at her thoughtfully as she took another bite of her sherbert. After flicking her ponytail off her shoulder and sitting up straighter, she said, "Her mom must be really sad."

"She is, honey."

She nodded to herself. "I'm glad you're helping look for her."

Mila smiled, a small measure of relief softening her shoulders. Harper was getting old enough to understand the importance of her job. That was something.

Back at the station, she pulled up the second video they had of the abduction. The one the trail cam caught. They'd gotten lucky when he used the only trail with a camera. It couldn't be someone familiar with that park, or they would've taken Coco on an unmonitored trail. There were two trails that led back to the parking lot plus a few unofficial ones.

She enlarged the image on her screen.

Is that you, Forester?

There were definitely a few curls peeking out of that hoodie and the limp that pointed toward him, but no other clues.

But why? Why would you take her? What is the motive?

There was no case without a motive.

Maybe he always wanted a daughter? No, he had the money and power to adopt quickly if that was the motive. And if it isn't Forester, what is the motive?

If a child is abducted and it's not a family member, it's usually a child predator. There was no sexual assault with Amelia. So, if it was the same abductor, at least Coco was probably safe from that particular horror.

But what if she's wrong? What if it's not the same abductor?

Then Coco could already be dead.

Mila shoved her keyboard forward in frustration.

"Detective Harlow?"

Mila glanced up at the young woman with wireframed glasses, her brown hair in layers, framing her face. "Yes?"

The woman held out a folder to her. "I'm part of the CART team, and we finished going through that list of names you gave us, cross-referencing the names in the Amelia Larson case with the names in Conly Parks's case."

Mila sat up, grabbed the folder and flipped it open. Scanning the top sheets she asked, "You have a match?"

Her eyes were shiny with excitement or hope. "We do."

Mila stared at the name highlighted on both sheets. "Roberto Torres." Her heart rate sped up. She didn't know who he was, but this was a significant break. "Thank you. You guys did great."

The woman smiled softly. "Good luck. I hope it helps."

Mila glanced around. Aiden emerged from the back of the bullpen, where the breakroom and lockers were. "Aiden!" she called, waving him over.

"What's up?" His gaze swept over her, worry pinching his mouth. His burgundy dress shirt was wrinkled, the sleeves pushed up.

She pressed the folder into his hand. "Did you interview a man named Roberto Torres?"

His expression hardened as he glanced down and read the name highlighted on both sheets. As he met her gaze again, his were full of questions. "Yeah, he works at Coco's school. Head Custodian. Why is he on Amelia Larson's list?"

"That's the question. First, let's see that interview." Mila dragged her chair over to his desk as he dropped into his chair.

Tension radiated from Aiden as he searched his desktop. "Here we go." He clicked open the interview file. "The mother said she saw Torres when she left Coco at the playground, so I did this interview myself."

"Oh, yeah, I remember her mentioning that now."

Aiden turned up the volume and leaned back. The video showed him sitting in interview Room Two, across from a wide-shouldered, dark-haired man in his fifties. The angle of the wall-mounted camera caught the back of Aiden's head and Torres's front. Torres was leaning forward, forearms resting on the table.

In the video, Aiden opened his leather binder. "I appreciate you coming in today. What is it you do at Garden Elementary, Mr. Torres?"

The man's voice was gruff, his speech pattern fast like he'd overdosed on caffeine. "I'm the head custodian. I help clean but also am in charge of schedules, ordering supplies, things like that."

Mila watched the man for any signs of nervousness. Besides his fast speech, there were no other tells. No fidgeting, no defensive posture.

"Were you acquainted with Conly Parks?"

Torres's right hand moved to rub the back of his neck. "Sure, I knew Coco, yeah. Being at the school every day, we get to know the kids, especially the friendly ones."

Mila's chest tightened. "Knew?" she whispered. It wasn't good when someone referred to the child in the past tense. She watched Aiden's head raise as he stared at the man. He'd caught it, too.

Aiden's tone was still friendly, but his spine had straightened. "Did you notice Coco being left at the playground after school?"

The man nodded deeply. "Well, sure. I was cleaning the B Wing classrooms. The playground is right behind those. I believe her mother waved at me, and I waved back."

Aiden jotted down notes on his steno pad. "Take me through your schedule after that."

Mila concentrated on Torres's mannerisms, and his demeanor as he easily reconstructed the next few hours of his time. Still relaxed. Still open. When Coco was taken, he said he was cleaning the gym bathrooms with the help of another custodian.

Aiden paused the video and turned to her. "I did verify this with the other custodian, that he was in the gym. It's across the campus." He shook his head. "He couldn't be in two places at once."

Mila stared at the monitor. "He also doesn't fit the physical description. I mean, he has the height but not the curly hair. And no limp?" She glanced at Aiden for confirmation. He shook his head. "But him being on Amelia's list, too, is a pretty big coincidence."

They both stared at the video, at the man sitting in their interview room. Was it possible they were looking at the kidnapper?

The noise and activity in the bullpen pulled her from her thoughts. Mila turned her attention to Aiden.

He was chewing on a thumbnail, probably beating himself up for not flagging this guy at the time and digging deeper.

"He seems pretty relaxed," she said. "Maybe that's because he has a solid alibi. Or maybe it's because he wasn't the one who actually took the girls." She cocked her head as a new thought formed. "What if he was working *with* the kidnapper? A partner. He could've alerted a partner that Coco had been left alone."

Aiden still chewed his thumbnail but nodded slowly. Finally, he dropped his hand and turned his chair toward her. "That would explain how the kidnapper got set up in the park so quickly to lure her to the fence." He rubbed his eyes with a frustrated groan. "Okay, the first question we need answered is why is Torres on Amelia Larson's list?"

"Agree. I need to pick up the case files from Detective Scott and find out." She jumped up and pulled her chair back to her desk. Catching the smirk Aiden shot her, she waved a finger at him. "You need a new hobby."

A gruff laugh escaped his throat. "I'll write up a warrant for Mr. Torres's phone records. See if he called anyone during the time Coco was on the playground alone."

"Great, get his financials, too. I'm betting if he was involved, money's his motive. Keep that devious mind of yours busy." She grabbed her phone off the desk and called Logan.

"Hello, Mila. Hungry?" Logan asked.

She could hear the smile in his voice, and she cursed her body for the heat it sent through her. She was hungry, but she wouldn't let herself think about the kind of hunger she experienced at the sound of his voice. "I could eat," she said, gathering her things, and tossing them into her leather bag. "I need to get the case files, there's been a development."

"I've got 'em in my truck. Meet me in Beachside Beat's parking lot in twenty."

Mila surveilled the parking lot as she waited for Logan, making sure she didn't see Paul's car. She really didn't want to run into him and Elly Prescott again, but she also wasn't going to let them dictate where she went for dinner.

Logan's truck swung into the space next to her, and he hopped out.

She met him at the tailgate as he popped it open and greeted her. "Hey. Figured you'd want to look at whatever lead you got before we grab a bite."

At the word *bite*, the memory of his teeth scraping down her neck last night came unbidden. She shoved it away. "Yeah, thanks." Sliding one of the boxes forward, she pulled off the lid. "Do you remember interviewing a man named Roberto Torres?"

His hands rested lightly on his hips. He shook his head. "Name isn't ringing a bell."

She pulled out a folder and flipped through it. "Well, he's the head custodian at Coco's school. For some reason he's on Amelia's list of acquaintances, too."

"Huh. All right, let's find him." Logan pulled a second box forward and started flipping through interview notes in the binders.

They worked in silence for fifteen minutes before Mila said, "Got it." She read the sheet of paper. "He's on the list of school employees. There's a handwritten note here that says, 'refused interview.'" She glanced up. "That's so weird. He was cooperative with us. And why is he on the employee list at Amelia's school when he works at Garden Elementary?"

He snapped his fingers. "Oh, I remember now. He had subbed at Amelia's school, Meadow View Elementary, at some point in the months leading up to her abduction. I'm pretty sure we didn't spend any time trying to push the interview because he had a solid alibi though."

Mila leaned her hip against the truck gate. "Yeah, one theory we came up with is that he may just be a partner or scout for the abductor. Having an alibi for the time of abduction wouldn't rule him out from being involved. Give me a sec."

Mila called Aiden and got him up to speed on Mr. Torres subbing at Amelia's school and refusing an interview. "Get him back in ASAP. Tonight, if possible. Text me when you have him."

Logan replaced the last lid on the boxes. "Let's get these moved to your truck and grab some food before you have to take off."

They settled in at the same table by the water. The temperature hovered in the mid-eighties, but a nice sea breeze cooled her skin. A burst of laughter from a table behind her had her jaw clenching. Her nerves were definitely on edge.

Taking a deep breath, she moved her attention to the sunlight sparkling on the surface of the water like a blanket of diamonds. The agitation prickling her mind began to calm down. Her chest loosened.

Better.

She met Logan's gaze. "If Torres called the kidnapper to tell them Coco was on that playground alone, it would explain how they got to her so quickly, right?" Logan gave her a curt nod. "It's easy to come up with a motive for him then. Money. The kidnapper could be paying him to find vulnerable girls, since he works in the school system and has access to them. Aiden's checking his financials. But that still doesn't give us motive for the kidnapper. What is he getting out of taking them?" She picked up an empty straw wrapper and twisted it around her finger. "Especially if Amelia's case is connected. He keeps her for three years and then kills her? No sexual assault. It makes no sense."

Logan's chin was perched on his fisted hands as he watched her. "There's no evidence the cases are connected, right?"

She pushed her hair behind her ears in frustration. "No, there's not. I shouldn't be trying to force these cases together. Maybe I'm doing that because I want it to be the same person. If they kept Amelia alive for that long, maybe they'll do the same with Coco, and we'll have a shot at bringing her back home alive." She took a long swig of her lemon water and sat the glass down harder than she meant to. "I just feel like we're missing something."

"Hey." He reached over and squeezed her hand. "I understand the urgency. But you have to give yourself a break. Take the next twenty minutes or so while we eat to clear your head. Go in fresh with Roberto Torres."

"You're right, thank you." She'd always had her biggest breakthroughs during a workout or long drive, when she wasn't trying to force her mind to add things up. Let the subconscious do its thing. That's the only advice her dad had given her when she'd first become a detective, and he gave that grudgingly. He was so against her becoming a cop, she wondered if he just didn't think she was capable. Her mom said he was just being overprotective. She didn't buy it.

The waitress brought their food. Mila forced herself to stay grounded in the present and enjoy the view as they ate and chatted about anything other than the case. At one point she watched Logan, thinking yeah, there's attraction there and he's smart, a little mysterious… but he's not Paul. Paul was her and Harper's home. And now Elly is sashaying around their sacred space.

She mentally shook herself. It hadn't worked with Paul. They'd tried. She needed to move on. Sometimes love just wasn't enough. Wasn't there a country song about that? Whatever, it was true, and she needed to put on her big girl panties and get the fuck over a relationship that was already over.

"You okay?" Logan's voice cut through her thoughts.

She jerked her head from the spot of nothing she was staring at. "Probably not," she whispered. Then she let herself meet his dark gaze, let her walls down just a little. "But I will be."

Thirty minutes in, she got a text from Aiden. She threw down her napkin. "They got him." She pushed back her chair, dug some cash out of her bag and slipped it under her plate.

"Keep me updated?" he asked as she rushed to gather her things.

"I will." Hopefully, she'd have some good news to tell him tonight.

FIFTEEN

Roberto Torres sat slumped forward in interview Room One, head down, dark hair with streaks of gray shining under the harsh fluorescent light.

Aiden, Frank, Mila and Captain Bartol watched him on the monitor. He'd been in there an hour and hadn't asked to leave or requested a lawyer. He'd only checked his phone once in a while and sipped the Mountain Dew they'd supplied.

They'd discussed strategy and decided they needed to be careful not to let him know he was a suspect until they could get more on him. If he shut down now, they'd lose their only chance. They were ready to go in.

Mila opened the door and walked in with a smile, shaking his hand. Aiden was right behind her. Aiden had already established a rapport with the suspect, so he would talk first. Mila slipped into the chair across from the small table, but Aiden moved the second chair around to sit right in front of Roberto with nothing between them.

"Sorry we had to interrupt your work tonight, Roberto." Aiden smiled easily. "You understand you can leave at any time?"

"It's okay, I want to help if I can." He pursed his lips, like he was stopping himself from saying more.

"We appreciate that." Aiden loosened the knot in his tie. "It's been a long day, as you can imagine." He casually turned and smiled at Mila. "I don't know about you, but I'm ready to see my girls." When she nodded in agreement, he turned back to Torres. "You married, Roberto? Any kids?"

The man's gaze dropped to the table. "Divorced. My twenty-two-year-old son is Army, stationed in Fort Irwin. Haven't seen him in eighteen months."

Aiden clicked his tongue in sympathy. "Hard when they leave the nest, huh? You live alone then?"

"Yeah."

Aiden flipped open his notepad and leaned closer, lowering his voice. "Just between us, we're starting to wonder if this case is related to the Amelia Larson case. You heard about that one?"

Roberto's eyes darted between Aiden and Mila, narrowing. "Sure. The girl who disappeared three years ago and was just found on Rattlesnake Island." He shook his head. "So awful. Hard to miss that kind of news. It's not like this is New York City, ya know? Kids are supposed to be safe here."

Aiden nodded slowly. "That's right, and it's come to our attention that you worked at Meadow View Elementary around that time, which is the school Amelia attended. So, we're wondering, maybe you witnessed something or someone important to that case and didn't realize it at the time."

"Oh." He shrugged, some tension leaving his shoulders. "I've worked there a few times, sure. Subbing when they're short-handed. Not just that school, we go where we're needed." He frowned, twirling the now empty soda can in his large hand. "I don't think I can remember back three years though. When I talked to a detective back then, I told him I didn't see anything."

Mila and Aiden shared a brief glance.

She kept the surprise out of her tone as she asked, "You talked to a detective?"

He leaned back in the chair. "Yeah, I can't remember his name. He came to the school. It was pouring down that day, and he was interviewing everyone in the cafeteria. I do get to know the kids at my permanent school, but since I was only a temp there, I didn't know the little girl Amelia. I wasn't very helpful."

"Will you excuse us a second?" Aiden rose from the chair and motioned to Mila.

They stood outside the interview room door, arms crossed, staring at each other.

"You think he's messing with us?" Aiden asked.

Mila's mouth opened, but she closed it and moved her attention to the door. "I honestly don't know what to think. There are no red flags there. He seems to believe what he says. There were at least a dozen detectives who helped with hundreds of interviews. I guess I could have missed his name in one of those files. But the note on the case specifically said he refused an interview."

"Maybe the note meant he refused a second interview? He said he talked to a detective in the cafeteria, maybe they asked him to come down to the station?"

"Maybe. Let's ask him."

They returned to their seats in the interview room.

"Did you ever get a call from another detective to come in for a second interview?" Mila asked, hoping to catch him off guard.

Something flashed in his dark eyes. Recognition? Irritation? Roberto poked his tongue inside his cheek and shook his head briefly. "After the lunchroom interview? Not that I remember."

Not that I remember. Good way to not answer the question without it being an outright lie. Were they underestimating him?

Mila clocked the slight shift in his demeanor. His arms crossed defensively; his lips pressed together. "So, you don't remember refusing to talk to a detective at Crystal Harbor PD?"

His eyes narrowed. "Refuse? That sounds like an accusation. Am I suspect? Do I need a lawyer?"

Mila watched him carefully. It was the first sign of discomfort he'd shown.

"We're just having a conversation, Mr. Torres," Aiden said quietly.

His head snapped toward Aiden, and he held out his palms. "I told you. I will help in any way I can. I just don't have any information. I'm sorry. I'd like to go now."

"Of course. You're free to go at any time." Aiden stood and stared down at the man. "One more question, Roberto. Do you own a boat?"

He scoffed, though the tension seemed to drain from his body as he eyed the door. "In my dreams."

"I hear you," Aiden said, smiling to reestablish a friendly vibe. He held out his card. "Thanks for coming in. If you do think of anything else, give me a call."

As they returned to the bullpen Mila said, "Let's hope something turns up on his phone records."

Aiden shoved a hand through his hair in frustration. "Yeah, think a call to the kidnapper would be asking too much?"

She shot him a weary smile. "Never hurts to ask."

She and Aiden brought Amelia's case file boxes back into the station. Then got to work, looking for Roberto's name in any other detective's notes.

After twenty minutes, Aiden held up a file. "Here it is. Detective Grant interviewed him in the school cafeteria as he said." He paused to read. "Torres said he didn't know Amelia. Was visiting his sister, Carmen Micheals, about thirty minutes away that evening. Alibi confirmed."

Mila rubbed her temples. "If he wasn't the abductor, just the scout, the alibi doesn't rule out his involvement."

Aiden nodded. "We need to recheck his alibi anyway. There's a phone number here for his sister, but I think I'll go see her in person. Get a feel for whether she'd protect her brother or not."

Captain Bartol emerged from her office. Her complexion was pale, and her bad knee was obviously bothering her as she limped over to them. "Anything?" she asked.

"Torres was interviewed at Meadow View Elementary after Amelia's disappearance and cooperated with that detective. But he doesn't remember being asked to come in for a second interview. I'm going to go talk to his alibi for Amelia's timeframe in person. It was his sister," Aiden said.

"And his alibi for Coco's timeframe?" she asked.

"A fellow janitor says they were cleaning the gym restrooms together." He shrugged. "There's no camera in there, so it's his word. Now that he's connected to both cases, we should get a more solid timeline for his activities that day. I'll get some uniforms to reinterview his colleagues."

"I'll call Sergeant Lockett and take care of that. You go talk to his sister." She turned to Mila, crossing her arms. "What's your gut say? You think these two cases are connected?"

Mila shared a startled glance with Aiden. Captain Bartol had never once asked about their gut feeling on any case. She only cared about the facts. She must be getting desperate.

Aiden shook his head in warning, but she had to speak her truth.

"I don't have any evidence of a connection," she said carefully.

"That wasn't my question, Detective," she stated with a raised brow.

Mila braced herself and then stepped out on the proverbial ledge. "My gut says that they are."

She held Mila's gaze, her mind turning. Then she nodded. "Then let's proceed like they are. Find the connection."

Mila's heart rate ticked up. "Yes, Captain."

—— ✳ ——

Mila needed a quiet place to think. She drove to the beach and parked, watching the steady roll of waves crash on shore through her windshield, and the towering white clouds shifting lazily in the wide-open sky. Then she took out her notebook and began to jot down all the possible connections, no matter how unlikely:

Age of both girls at the time of abduction was the same. Forester's interest in them. The fact that Coco was taken so soon after Amelia was found. Torres working at both schools. Did Torres have a connection with Forester?

And then she remembered what Logan had said. Both girls had been put in danger at home.

She stared back out the windshield, but her mind was focused inward.

Coco had a social media page, so the perp could have noticed her there, noticed all the adult men following and commenting on her photos. Recognized the danger. But what about Amelia? She didn't have social media. How would her kidnapper know about Amelia being shot by Cole Richards, her mother's boyfriend?

She adjusted the computer terminal to face her, pulled up Google and typed in 'Cole Richards.' There were a few articles about his arrest, but none of them mentioned Amelia's name.

Did that mean the kidnapper knew Amelia personally?

She jotted down that question and circled it. She needed to go through Amelia's case file again and reinterview the people closest to her. Also, Torres could have heard about the shooting from other employees at Meadow View Elementary. A child being shot wouldn't escape small-town gossip.

A sudden knock on her window startled her out of her thoughts. Turning quickly, she saw Elly's bright smile, her blonde hair free and blowing in the breeze like a goddamn supermodel. Groaning to herself, she pressed the window down button. "Elly. What can I do for you?"

Elly pulled off her Gucci leopard print sunglasses and met Mila's eyes. "I know this is awkward with me dating Paul. I just wanted to say I hope one day it won't be. I think we could be friends."

Mila kept her expression neutral, even as the heat crawled up her neck to her cheeks. "Is Paul feeding you inside information? Is that how you got to the dock so quickly when Amelia's body was discovered?"

A shadow of a smile flitted across her face. "I would think you'd know Paul better than that."

She had to stop herself from picturing exactly how well *Elly* knew Paul. "Who then? Who tipped you off?"

"I would also think you know better than to think I'd give up my sources."

Mila's jaw ached from clenching her teeth. "We'll find the leak." She shoved the SUV in reverse. "And I don't think being friends is in the cards for us." She hit the gas, getting a little bit of satisfaction when Elly had to step back quickly from the window.

As she drove back to the station, she let out a long sigh. God, she hated the way Elly brought out the worst in her. This jealousy was like a sore in her soul. She had to find a way to heal it, to be okay with whoever Paul dated.

Paul. Time to tell him about the poisoned hotdogs Kittie found in the yard. Before she got out of the car at the station, she shot him a text: *We need to talk.*

His reply came immediately: *I'll call you tonight*

At her desk, she'd watched both videos of Coco's kidnapping over and over. She sat staring at a still frame from the trail camera where the black and white image had caught the kidnapper mid-stride, Coco's small hand in his, her other hand clutching the Barbie doll.

Who are you? And why did you take her?

The lack of motive was really starting to get to her.

Frank strolled over and stood behind her. "Not sure releasing that image to the public was a help or not. Especially with the reward sitting at ten grand now. So many people have called in swearing that's their neighbor or husband, boyfriend, co-worker."

She swiveled her chair around to look up at him. "One of them may be right."

He grunted and adjusted his glasses. "Aiden filled me in on the Roberto Torres interview before he left to talk to the sister. So, we're thinking he could be involved somehow?"

She reached for her water bottle. "It's a theory. Maybe he didn't grab Coco himself, but alerted the person who did that she was left alone." She took a sip and shrugged. "If Torres was some kind of scout for the kidnapper, he'd probably have been around the festival at the same time as Amelia. I've asked Matt to recheck the footage for any sign of him."

Frank snorted. "Poor Matt. I'm sure he's planning your demise as we speak." He leaned against her desk, his smile fading. "Forester is still my bet. He has the limp, the right height and curly hair. And he's obsessed with little girls. You think they know each other? Him and Torres?"

"No idea how they would. They move in different circles," Mila said. "But can't rule it out."

Frank's eyes darkened. "If Forester's family money didn't have such a chokehold on this town, we'd already be in there ripping his mansion apart looking for that little girl."

"Maybe. Maybe not. There's still not enough for probable cause." She crossed her arms and looked up at Frank. "Have we called the local boat rental places for their records the week Amelia was dumped?"

Frank shrugged. "Don't know if anyone got to it. I'll check." He pushed off her desk and went back to his own.

Turning back to her monitor, she Googled Roman Forester and scrolled through the images. There were more than a few of him at fancy venues, dressed up, arms around other rich people holding champagne glasses. None she could find on his yacht. A bunch in art galleries, standing stoically in front of his paintings, all showcasing little girls. If what he'd explained to her was true, then how did he get so obsessed with "elevating the feminine" as he put it?

There's only one person who would know. She gathered her things and headed to her car. If this was harassment, so be it. She had a little girl to find.

SIXTEEN

Coco

Tears soaked the pillow beneath Coco's face. She whisper-sang the theme song to *Frozen,* like her mom did for her when she couldn't fall asleep at night. Only she wasn't even sure if it was night or day. One arm was wrapped tightly around a teddy bear she'd named Peaches, her index finger stroking his glass eye over and over in a self-soothing motion. A while ago, she had gotten really scared and banged on the door for a long time, screaming for her mom.

But no one came.

Now she was just sad, and her palms still stung. She knew her mom was going to be so mad at her. She got mad when she got worried. She might take away her movie time again.

Coco sniffled and then a terrible thought bubbled up like a monster whispering inside her head. *What if the man is lying? What if he isn't going to let her go home?*

A whimper worked its way up her throat, and she suddenly had to pee.

She pushed herself up and went to the plastic toilet. As she sat there, she looked around the room. She'd been so busy playing with the boxes of new Barbies, she hadn't thought about getting herself home.

Pulling up her leggings, she decided she needed to be brave. Like Elsa.

Wiping at her still-damp cheeks, she moved slowly around the room, not knowing exactly what she was looking for. A magic portal would be nice. One that she could jump into and come out the other side into her own bedroom. A small smile tugged at the corner of her mouth as she imagined how she would surprise her mom. But at the thought of her mom, the smile disappeared and an ache began in her chest.

She pushed on all the walls in case there was a secret door. Then she lay on pink rectangular rug in front of the bed and stared up at the ceiling. "Please help me," she whispered to the room. "I need to go home."

When there was no answer, she turned over on her belly, now eye-level with the space beneath the small bed. She pulled herself forward as she noticed scratches on the wood floor.

Her small finger ran across the letters, sounding them out loud. "A.M.E.L.I.A."

Seventeen

The maid tipped her nose in the air, her lips turning down. "Mr. Forester is not here."

"That's okay. I actually came to speak with Mrs. Forester." Mila took advantage of the woman's confusion and stepped around her, moving quickly into the living room she'd waited in on her first visit.

"Detective!" the maid called behind her. "She cannot be disturbed."

Mila let out a breath of relief. Mrs. Forester was here. Sitting in front of the fireplace in her wheelchair just like before. Only there was another woman in the room in a nurse's outfit, sitting on the sofa, writing in a file. She stood, startled when Mila entered.

Mila held up her badge. "I just need a few minutes of Mrs. Forester's time."

Mrs. Forester turned to her, eyes widening. But they quickly crinkled in the corners as she smiled. "A visitor. Come in." She waved a bony hand, her diamond bracelet sparkling in the firelight. Her other hand was resting in her lap. No sign of the doll she'd been previously cradling in her lap.

"I don't know if that's a good idea." The nurse's gaze flicked from her patient to Mila, her lips pursed in disapproval.

"Nonsense," Mrs. Forester's weak voice called from across the room. "This is still my house, and I want to speak to my visitor. You can leave us alone."

Mila noticed she seemed more coherent today. Good.

The nurse shot Mila a heavy side-eye as she passed, calling behind her, "I'll give you ten minutes."

Mrs. Forester maneuvered the chair away from the fire and motioned for Mila to take a seat on the sofa. When she did, the woman settled her wheelchair a few feet from her. "I must confess, you remind me of an old friend of mine, Cece from Spain, with that dark hair and beautiful green eyes. But I don't remember if we've met."

Mila smiled. "Detective Harlow. You can call me Mila."

"Mila. To what do I owe the pleasure of your company?"

She decided to get to the point since she didn't know how long the staff would tolerate her presence. "We have a little girl missing. Your son is connected to the case, and I'd like to clear him of suspicion so we can move on. Can you help me do that?"

Her mouth turned down in concern. "Oh, dear. I can try."

Mila leaned forward, creating a more intimate space between them. "Your son's artwork is centered mainly around little girls. Can you help me understand his obsession with them?"

"Oh." She chuckled, her frail shoulders relaxing. "Well, because he is one."

Mila blinked hard. "I don't understand."

"No, I don't suppose anyone does. Not really." Her cloudy gray eyes grew damp and unfocused. "When he was four, he told us he was a girl and wanted dolls for Christmas. Of course, his father had a conniption and gave him a black eye. Forbid him to ever speak those words again." Her head wobbled with what looked like residual anger. "I, on the other hand, would let him wear dresses and play with my makeup when his father was out of town. By six he wanted me to call him Ramona. He was so happy when his father was away, and he could be himself. He would dance around the house, singing and giggling like the little ball of joy he was." Her thin lips curved into a wistful smile. "He loved art, too. Even at that young age. So, I got him private art lessons, and we'd sit by the pool together drawing and painting, having tea parties and wearing whatever the hell we wanted." Her face crumpled with old grief. "One day his dad came home early. He was absolutely horrified. Beat both of us black and blue and then locked Ramona up in her room for a month, no contact with anyone."

She paused and squeezed her eyes closed, like she couldn't bear to relive that day, even in her memory. "Until Ramona broke and placed all her female items, everything that was her identity, in a trash bag and willingly threw them out. She will always be my Ramona. But to Roman, she's the little girl locked away inside him. Never to be let out."

Locked away. An interesting way to put it. "Even after his father passed?"

"He already had his identity as Roman by then. It was too late." Her frail shoulders lifted slightly, watery eyes flashing with defiance. "I must confess, I enjoyed having a daughter for a time. My dead husband can't take away those memories we made."

Would Roman have taken a little girl for his mother? So she could have a daughter again? Mila glanced up at the ceiling. How many rooms were up there? She wanted to ask if she could search the place, but she couldn't risk it without a warrant. Roman could come home at any time and stop the search.

Instead, she placed a hand on the woman's bony forearm and gave it a squeeze. "You were very helpful, Mrs. Forester. Thank you for your time."

Back at the station, she started over with Amelia's case. Going back to the night the little girl was shot in the arm. She revisited the hospital records and the arrest records for Cole Richards. The arresting officer had been Bart Terrance. She paused. What if Logan was right? What if Amelia had been taken because of some sense of twisted vigilante justice?

Maybe Officer Terrance took her to keep her out of the home where she'd been shot. But then why keep her for three years just to kill her? It didn't make sense.

She picked up the phone anyway, called Safety Harbor PD and asked for the records department. After a brief hold, she was told Officer Terrence had moved to Chicago a year ago.

She hung up. So much for that theory. She was reaching now. Guessing. She didn't have time for that.

Torres was a viable suspect, but Aiden had that covered for now. Forester wasn't in the clear. She needed to focus on getting something on him. Something that would give them probable cause to search that damn house.

Her phone buzzed. It was Kittie. "Everything okay?"

"Not sure. There's a strange man here. Roman Forester. He's asking for you."

Mila almost choked on her heart which was suddenly in her throat. "At the house?"

"Yes."

She jumped up, sending her desk chair flying behind her and grabbed her bag. "Where is he now?"

"On the porch, just sitting."

"Keep the doors locked, keep Harper inside, and keep an eye on him. Call me back if he moves. I'm on my way."

It only took her ten minutes to pull into her driveway and park next to his Rolls. Sure enough, Roman sat on her front porch, legs crossed, looking like he didn't have a care in the world.

She kept her gaze locked on him, her hand resting near her Glock as she moved up the steps.

Roman eyed her hand. "No need for that, Detective. I just brought you what you asked for, the names of anyone I think may be trying to set me up."

Mila didn't buy that explanation and didn't move her hand. "You couldn't email them to me?"

He sighed, his gaze moving back out to the gulf waters. "This is a lovely view."

When he didn't say anything else, she moved to sit in the wicker chair next to him and waited for him to get to the point of his visit.

His voice was strained and low as he said, "Mother told me you two had a nice chat about me."

Ah, so that was it. Was he here to threaten her? "Yes, we did. And I'm sorry you had to hide who you really are."

His stormy gray eyes assessed her, and he seemed to accept her comment as sincere with a nod. "Do you know my father threatened to have me castrated? So I couldn't poison his family line with my depravity." Whatever wall he kept up abruptly fell, and he let her see the raw pain behind the mask. "Isn't that ironic?"

People in pain caused pain in others. Pain was dangerous. "Why are you here?"

He scooted forward in the chair and pinned her with his stare like a butterfly to a board. "I've noticed the sheriff's cars following me. I just want to assure you you're wasting your time on me. I wouldn't kidnap a child. Or hurt them."

"That's something a kidnapper would say."

He threw back his head and laughed. Then tilted his head and gave her a nod. "I like you, Detective. Let me know if there's anything I can do so you stop wasting time and resources focusing on me."

As he stood up, she said, "You could let us search your house."

He stared at her while contemplating something. "I think my lawyer would have a coronary. But... then again, he does work for me. I'll talk to him." He handed her a sheet of folded paper. "I'll let you get back to it."

Before he reached the bottom step, she called out, "Hey, do you know Roberto Torres? He said he was a friend of yours."

He stopped and turned slowly back to face her. His gray eyes were glowing with something different now. Curiosity? Challenge? "Not off the top of my head. Who is he, may I ask?"

The corners of Mila's mouth lifted. "You may."

His answering smile stretched wider. "But you're not going to reply. Must mean he's a suspect, no?" When he realized Mila wasn't going to give him anything he adjusted the necklaces at his throat and chuckled. "I'd say good luck, Detective, but I don't think you'll need it."

Kittie was waiting for her just inside the door, looking concerned. "Everything okay?"

"Fine." She gave Kittie a distracted hug. "Where's Harp?"

"I sent her up to her room."

At the sound of her mother's voice, Harper barreled down the stairs, Oscar scrambling down behind her.

"Mom! Who was that?" Harper asked as she wrapped her arms around Mila's waist.

"No one important." Mila squeezed her back, then said, "I just need to make a phone call, and then I want to hear all about your day, okay?"

Harper released Mila and then rolled her eyes. "Hannah had boy drama."

"Boy drama?" Mila grimaced at Kittie.

Kittie fought a grin then took Harper's hand, leading her into the kitchen. "Let's give your mom's heart a break and go make a snack."

Mila pulled out her cell and called Captain Bartol. She eyed the two names on the sheet of paper Forester had given her. Yeah, he definitely could've emailed this.

"Hey, Cap. Roman Forester just showed up on my doorstep. Gave me two names of people he thinks might set him up. Also said he's willing to talk to his lawyer about letting us search his place without a warrant."

Captain Bartol scoffed. "No lawyer in their right mind would allow that."

Mila refolded the paper and shoved it into her slack's pocket. "No, and he knows that. He's working real hard to get off our radar."

"Sounds like we need to up the pressure. Maybe he'll make a mistake. Let me see if I can find room in the budget for twenty-four-hour surveillance. At least for a few days, in case he tries to move anything from the house."

⁎

Mila and Paul had played phone tag last night, never connecting. So, as she drove back to the station, she tried again.

"Hey," he answered over the loud voices crackling through his radio. "On a call, but what do you need?"

What does she need? Well, that's a loaded question. She decided this wasn't the right time for a conversation about Elly. "Your shift ends at eleven?"

"Yeah."

"You have plans?"

"I do, but I'll be in Edgewater if you need me."

"Can you drop by the house and check on Harper?"

There was a pause and then, "Something wrong?"

"Roman Forester showed up at the house a bit ago."

"Did he threaten you?" Paul growled.

"No. I just don't feel comfortable with him knowing where I live. I won't be going home anytime soon, so I'd just feel better if you check in on Harper and your mom."

"Yeah, no problem. He's a person of interest?"

Normally she wouldn't hesitate to share this with him. But Elly has made her unsure whether she can trust him now. And Mila resented her the most for that. "We're still looking into him. Also, your mom found hotdogs laced with rat poison in the yard. We're assuming that's what made him sick."

After a brief, shocked silence, his voice exploded over the line. "What? Someone poisoned Oscar on purpose? Do you think it was Forester?"

"Yeah, looks like it was on purpose. But I honestly don't have a clue who it could be."

Paul's voice grew muffled as he talked to someone in his presence. "Look, I gotta go, but we do have a few things to talk about. I'll call you later."

Mila gripped the steering wheel as she disconnected the call. Elly lives in Edgewater. Of course he was going to be with her tonight. They were spending an awful lot of time together. Was this getting serious? Was he going to ask her soon if he could introduce her to Harper? Is that what he wanted to talk to her about? She shook her head and turned up the radio. Not going to go there.

You have enough to worry about without worrying about things that haven't happened yet.

She forced her attention back to the investigation. Forester hadn't given anything away when she'd asked if he knew Roberto Torres. They needed to ask Torres if he knew Forester. Could they get lucky enough to find a call to Forester from Torres? She scoffed at the thought. That would be too easy, and this case had been anything but easy. As soon as they got Torres's phone records, they'd bring him back in.

It was almost midnight when a text came in from Paul that all was quiet at the house. She'd spent the last few hours sitting at her desk researching people, including the two names Forester had given her. One was an art gallery owner, and one was a local politician. She didn't think either one of them had anything to do with the abductions. But she'd talk to them in person tomorrow anyway. Leave no stone unturned and all that.

She threw her pen on the desk and stretched her arms and neck, glancing around the room. The blinds were closed, but she could sense the darkness pressing against them from outside. Captain Bartol had left about an hour ago. She'd be back at six AM to lead the morning team meeting.

Aiden was at his desk, working on reports on the interviews so far. Frank was following up on tipline calls, and Matt was in his office going through the Safety Harbor Seafood Festival video footage for any sign of Forester or Torres. Nighttime brought a different kind of energy. More subdued but no less pressing.

It had been three days since Coco's abduction. Three days and no good leads. No body, either, even after all the dumpsters in the area were searched, so that was the only bright spot right now. The little girl could still be alive.

If so, where was he keeping her?

As she took a sip of cold coffee, she let her mind wander back to Paul, and their first few months together. They'd stolen every moment that they could. He had been like a drug. She couldn't get enough of him. She'd had crushes before, but Paul was the first man who'd consumed her every waking thought. Does Elly feel the same? Is Paul giving Elly everything he'd given her in the beginning?

Mila's gut twisted and a sudden desperate ache clutched her heart. She pressed her palm against her chest. Her therapist had warned her she needed to deal with her feelings about the divorce, talk about what would happen when Paul met someone else. Mila had told her she'd cried enough and was moving on. But had she? The pain felt exactly the same right now. The intensity dialed up to a hundred. A few long seconds ticked by, and she realized she couldn't take a deep breath. Was she having a heart attack? She breathed through the squeezing pain.

No. It was a panic attack.

Oh, God. It had been nine years since she'd had one, but the familiar terror now held her in its brutal grip. The edges of her vision went dark.

"Mila!"

She lifted her head at the sound of her name. She must've stood up at some point, and she was clutching the edge of her desk, trying to suck in air, in a full-blown panic.

Aiden was in front of her, grasping her arms, his voice far away like it was floating down a tunnel. She couldn't focus on anything except getting her lungs to expand so she could get some oxygen.

She felt the pressure Aiden was exerting on her shoulders until her backside hit the chair. Then a paper bag was slipped over her mouth and nose.

Aiden's calm voice was close to her ear. "Just breathe. In. Out."

Someone on her other side pressed a damp paper towel to the back of her neck. She was still clutching her chest, trying to keep her heart from bouncing out. Her body buzzed like live wires were running through it.

"In. Out. That's it," Aiden repeated calmly.

Eventually, her lungs opened and the black tunnel around her vision receded. Aiden's voice pulled her back into the room. She blinked up at him through a sheen of tears and nodded.

He slowly removed the bag, leaned against the desk and rubbed his forehead. "You okay?"

She glanced from him to Frank, who was holding the damp paper towel, his own pupils blown wide by fear behind his glasses. She hated looking weak in front of him. He didn't do well with women's emotions. His terror almost made her laugh, but she didn't want them to worry about her mental health any more than they were right now.

She took one long deep breath, satisfied with the way it filled the bottom of her lungs, and then blew it out. "I'm fine, guys." She suddenly felt claustrophobic and needed to get out of there. "You know what, I'm just going to go home and grab a shower, regroup." Her legs felt like jelly and her hands were shaking as she pushed herself up and started gathering her things. She knew Aiden noticed.

"Try to grab a couple of hours of sleep, too," Aiden said. "We'll be here, and we'll call you if anything important comes up."

"Thanks." She glanced over at Frank, who was still watching her wearily. "And stop looking at me like I have two heads, Frank," she snapped.

He raised an eyebrow. "Have you checked the mirror?"

"Asshole," she said with a gruff laugh.

As soon as she stepped out into the warm night air, she let her head fall back and inhaled another deep breath. Dark clouds diffused the moonlight, and a tropical breeze dried the sweat on the back of her neck. It was a beautiful evening, but there was no time to enjoy it.

She slid into the leather seat, started the SUV and released everything she'd been fighting. The frustration and fear of not finding Coco. The jealousy and confusion around what Paul still meant to her. Worry about Harper's mental health. Her chest heaved. Tears rolled down her cheeks, her neck and then her collarbone. She reached into her console to find takeout napkins and wiped at her face and neck.

"Damn it, Mila. Get your shit together," she growled into the dark SUV's cab. She threw her head back against the seat, bounced it a few times, and then closed her eyes.

Immediately, she was taken back to the day she'd met Paul at the police academy.

She'd arrived at the first class thirty minutes early and took a seat up front. Paul was five minutes behind her. He slid into the seat right next to her. At the sound of the chair scraping, she lifted her gaze, planning on giving the person a polite smile and greeting. But she had ended up doing a double take at the built, confident, intense man holding her gaze. It had taken her a full thirty seconds staring into the most captivating ice-blue eyes she'd ever seen before she could breathe out a *hi*.

He nodded and when he spoke, it was also a whisper. *Hey*. It was one word, but it was full of the same flavor of emotions she was feeling. Intrigue, attraction, surprise. They were immediately inseparable.

When her awareness came back to the present, a light rain had started. She hit the windshield wipers and smeared the sprinkles in an arc. The pain began to solidify into anger. She needed an outlet for this pain. She could go home and hit the bag for an hour. That'd probably wake up the house. Or...

Anything you need.

She could purge Paul from her damn brain. Before she could change her mind, she threw the SUV into drive and hit the gas.

Eighteen

Twenty minutes later she was pulling into Detective Scott's driveway, second-guessing herself. It wasn't raining here, but a thick layer of dark clouds blocked any moonlight. No streetlights. No house lights. Everything was dark and quiet. It was almost one in the morning, of course, he'd be asleep.

She chewed on her thumbnail, letting the SUV idle.

Maybe she should just go home and take a cold shower. What if she had misread his signals? Yeah, this was a bad idea.

As she grabbed the shifter, movement caught the corner of her eye.

She glanced over at the front door and her heart skipped a beat.

The door was now opened. Logan stood there in a pair of low-slung black sweatpants, his arms crossed as he leaned against the doorframe, waiting for her decision. With no shirt, she could see the outline of his broad shoulders and muscular chest in the shadows. Something low in her belly stirred. She could feel the pull of release, the promise of silencing her mind.

She shut off the engine and opened the door. As she walked toward him, his face was unreadable, but his eyes burned with intensity. She stood before him and lifted her chin to gaze into his eyes. There was no mistaking the heat there. The heady scent of his soap and the warmth of his bed radiated from him.

"Mila—"

She reached up and pressed her index finger against his lips. Talking isn't what she came for.

His mouth shifted into a knowing smirk beneath her fingertip as he reached up, took her hand and then tugged her into his house. The door shut. Her back was pressed up against it, Logan's hard, warm body at her front. His lidded brown eyes held hers, while his hands gripped her hips. He leaned in and softly pressed his lips against hers.

He was being gentle. Too gentle. She immediately leaned forward, greedy for more.

This time he gave her what she wanted as he moved a hand to the back of her neck and growled as their lips met. Tongues sliding against each other, teeth clashing, soft sighs of pleasure.

Yes. This is what she needed. To get lost for just a little while. To forget.

God, he tasted good. Like mint and whiskey. Like danger and oblivion.

She moaned into his mouth and that seemed to be too much for him. He slid his arm beneath her legs and swept her off the ground. Her stomach dropped like she was on a rollercoaster. She wrapped her arms around his neck, enjoying being pressed against his heated, bare chest as he carried her into his bedroom, their mouths still exploring each other.

They landed on the bed together, and Mila let everything fall from her mind... Paul, the kidnapping, the murder, every burden she carried on her shoulders fled under this man's touch until she was nothing but heavy breathing, electrified nerve endings, and her mind a blissful void.

A few hours later, she blinked awake, quickly taking in her surroundings. Her cheek lay on Logan's bare chest, and he was mumbling in his sleep. A deep, sorrowful noise escaped from his throat, and he thrashed, suddenly jolting awake. She pushed herself up and watched him. When he became aware of the room and her worried gaze, he raked a hand down his face. "Sorry. Nightmare."

Mila squeezed his blanketed thigh. She had a feeling if she could grab the edge of this man's darkness and peel it back, what she'd find would be a festering, open wound. But today was not the day to explore that with him. "I have to get back to the station. Can I use your shower?" Hopefully, an ice-cold shower would wake her up, since she'd only got about thirty minutes of sleep.

He let his head drop back onto the pillow and threw a forearm over his eyes, a sheet covering him from the waist down. A low chuckle vibrated in his throat. "My body, my shower, whatever you need, darlin'."

"Such a southern gentleman," she teased, slipping out of the bed and gathering her clothes from the floor.

The mattress squeaked as he shifted. When she glanced back, his dark gaze glittered. "I thought I just spent two hours showing you how ungentlemanly I can be."

Despite her mood falling as the real world came back into focus, she smiled. Relief was the prominent emotion she felt. Relief that she wasn't broken as a woman, that she could still feel passion and enjoy a man's touch. It had been five long years since she'd let a man touch her. Guilt slithered into her mind like a shadow along with the thought of Paul.

Damn it. No, he was not going to ruin this for her.

With her gathered clothes pressed against her chest, she stopped and stared at a framed family photo on Logan's dresser. The only personal touch she'd seen in his home. "Is this you as a boy?" she asked, leaning closer to study the tall, lanky boy in the dim lighting. "And your family?" A man had his arm slung over the boy. A woman had both her arms wrapped around the shoulders of a young girl.

"Yeah."

"How old were you here?"

"Ten."

She glanced back at him when she heard the raw ache in his tone. He didn't offer any more information.

Maybe he was estranged from them. Or they were no longer alive. She was lucky she still had her parents. A story for another day, she thought. She stepped into the bathroom and closed the door before flicking on the light. As she turned on the spray of water, she noticed two black bottles of men's shampoo and body wash. Great, she was going to smell like him all day.

Shivering from standing in the shower for ten minutes, letting the ice-cold water soak into her bones, she stepped out onto the squishy bathmat and glanced around. She'd forgotten a towel.

Opening the door, she didn't see Logan in bed anymore. "Logan?"

No answer.

With water dripping down her body and leaving puddles on the floor, she opened the closet door and flipped on the light. Dress pants, jeans and a few suit jackets to the right, polos and T-shirts on the left. Boxes and a shoe rack were stacked along the back wall. *Bingo.* Black towels sat on the top shelf. She stepped in and pulled one off the shelf, rubbing it over her hair and body.

To her right, a guitar leaned against the wall. Next to that was a plastic shelf with an old record player, a remote-control car, a drone, and an old Atari console. His hobbies. She smiled, feeling like she was seeing the boy inside the man. Her gaze went back to the drone.

The drone, that's it.

She remembered when the FAA started requiring all drones to be registered. That meant there was a database. They could pull up all registered drone owners in the area. She felt a surge of hope.

"Mila?" Logan called.

She wrapped the towel around her and stepped out of the closet. "Just finding a towel."

He leaned against the doorframe, his intense gaze starting at her bare legs and traveling up to her face. "If you want to make it back to the station, I suggest you put some clothes on." He winked. "I have coffee for you to go."

Aiden turned in his desk chair as she pulled open her drawer to shove her bag in. "Get some...?" He paused, his eyes sweeping over her. He folded his arms. "Aren't those the same clothes you were wearing when you left? You didn't get any rest, did you?"

She glanced down at the clothes that had betrayed her and then at her teammate, who was too damn perceptive for his own good. "None of your business, Reyes." She plopped down in her chair and wiggled her mouse, hoping he'd leave it.

No such luck.

Aiden pushed his roller chair around her desk until it was beside hers, staring at her profile. "Your hair's damp, so you obviously showered." He wheeled a few inches closer and sniffed, then made a show of gasping and covering his mouth. "Oh my god. You little hussy. Let me guess. Detective Scott?"

"Don't be a teenager," she growled, refusing to look at him.

He held his hands up with a grin she could see from her peripheral. "No judgment here. I'm actually happy for you."

She finally moved her gaze to him, fighting a smile, and lifted a brow. "Are you done?"

His eyes sparkled, and he did look happy for her, even with the dark half-moons beneath them. He laughed, leaning back in his chair. "Not even close."

"You're an idiot," she snorted. "Anyway... I thought of something tonight." She pulled up the FAA website. "We can get a list of registered drones in our area."

"Good idea but more lists, yah," he said sarcastically.

While she looked up the contact number on the FAA website, Aiden filled her in on the last few hours she'd missed. "Matt and Frank took off a bit ago. Matt found a man who could be Forester on one of the Seafood festival videos someone had turned in. He has the height and the limp. His hair is shorter and hidden under a baseball cap, but there's no good angle of his face to make a positive ID. Frank has an impossible list of leads to follow up on tomorrow from the tipline." He swiveled back and forth in his chair. "Oh, he also found the detective who followed up on the boat rental companies in the area and got a million-page list of renters in the last week."

Mila shot him a grin as she lifted her desk phone receiver to leave a message for the FAA's law enforcement assistance program. "A million pages, huh?"

"Okay. A few hundred, but Christ, I feel like we're drowning in lists."

She left a message and then blew out a breath and really looked at Aiden. His brown waves were sticking up from him shoving his hand through in frustration all night, his face was drawn and pale. "I know." She glanced at the clock on her computer. "Why don't you go home and grab a power nap, kiss your girls? The chaos starts again in two hours at the seven AM meeting.

"Yeah, all right. I'll stop by your mom's place and grab us the good stuff on my way back."

"That'd be great." Mila took a swallow from the warm water bottle she'd left on her desk, scooted her chair forward and opened the browser that still held her search for "six-year-old girl" "birthday" and "abducted." She drummed her fingers on the desk as she scanned the results.

Well, neither Amelia nor Coco were abducted on their birthday. And it was only Amelia's case that had anything to do with a birthday crown. That wasn't relevant in Coco's case. Still… it meant something in Amelia's case. So, if the cases were connected, it meant something to both.

She clicked on the article about the six-year-old girl, Sheena Garcia, fighting off an abductor in a Miami Walmart by clamping her teeth down on his thigh as she kicked items off the shelf to alert her mom, who was at the end of the aisle

"Good for you," Mila whispered into the quiet bullpen. She shivered.

The other end of the aisle?

These pedos were getting bold. The article mentioned it was Sheena's birthday. and she was there to pick out a toy. Nothing of relevance.

Mila moved on to the next article from Florida.

This one was grim. A three-year-old had been abducted from a birthday party in Tampa. Ashley Green. Her body had been found two weeks later in the trunk of an abandoned car. Cause of death suffocation.

That could be the same cause of death as Amelia. They would never know.

She opened another browser and researched the case. Her frustration mounted. The man had been caught and was serving a thirty-year sentence.

Not our guy.

For the next hour, she read every article she could find about any little girl's death or abduction in Florida. When nothing fit, she broadened her search to the whole US.

Her eyes were burning by the time voices and footsteps sounded behind her. It was quarter to six. She turned, hoping it was Aiden with fresh coffee. But it was Captain Bartol and the CART commander, Ed Yarnell.

"Good morning," the captain said, stopping by her desk as Ed continued into her office. "Any leads last night?"

Mila filled her in on the call she'd placed to the FAA to get a list of drones registered in the area.

She nodded and squeezed Mila's shoulder. "May today be the day."

"Yes, ma'am." She knew this was as close to a prayer as the captain would get.

When Aiden sat a steaming coffee and protein muffin on her desk fifteen minutes later and mumbled a sleepy good morning, she was staring at a ten-year-old Houston Chronicle article: *Magnolia Farms Honors Daughter on the Twentieth Anniversary of Her Death.*

It was an article about the family's charity helping other families who had lost a child. Mila's attention was caught on one line: *Magnolia Scott tragically fell from a tree and died on her sixth birthday.* There was a photo of an elderly couple holding up a photo of a little girl.

Magnolia Scott. Scott? Could they be related to Logan? Could this be Logan's little sister?

That would be a huge coincidence. Maybe not his sister but a relative? She tried to enlarge the image, but it just made it pixely. It kind of resembled the little girl in the family photo on his dresser. Thirty years ago? The timeline fit. And Texas? Yeah, Logan's accent could be Texan. But what does this mean?

She leaned back in the chair and forced her tired brain to focus.

Okay, Logan's sister—or possibly another relative—maybe died in a tragic accident on her birthday. Her sixth birthday.

Why had he never mentioned that?

Well, it's not like you traded heartbreaks. You didn't tell him about your attack in college, either. But this is different. Right?

The girls hadn't been taken on their birthday, but Amelia had been left with a birthday crown. That's just an open invitation for Logan to tell her about losing his sister on her birthday. Maybe he just doesn't talk about it. Or maybe he's not related to this family at all.

She'd have to stop speculating and just ask him. Tonight. Right now she had to get ready for the morning briefing.

Mila spent the day helping Frank run down the most viable leads the tip line had brought in, interviewing the people she could find, and leaving messages for the people she couldn't. She managed to stop by home and eat dinner with Kittie and Harper, which was the highlight of her day, before she returned to the daunting task of leads.

She also stopped by and visited Coco's mother to see how she was holding up.

Raelynn had taken a leave of absence from work and looked like she hadn't slept since the day her daughter disappeared. Not that Mila could blame her. All she could do was promise her there were hundreds of people looking for her daughter.

The damn clock was ticking so loud she couldn't hear herself think.

At six o'clock, Aiden was back from talking to Torres's sister. She didn't change her story. Still gave him an alibi. But Aiden also found out that the visit was out of the blue, and they usually only see each other on holidays. So, maybe he purposely gave himself an alibi.

At seven Roberto Torres's phone records and financials were in their possession. Mila took the phone records and Aiden took the financials.

Mila was looking for any calls or texts the day Coco was abducted. Unfortunately, there was only one call at 5:54 PM. Mila dialed it.

"Franco's Pizza, can you please hold."

She hung up and said, "Hey, Aiden." When he turned around with a raised brow she asked, "What are the odds someone at Franco's Pizza is the abductor?"

"How long was the call?"

She glanced at the sheet. "Nine minutes."

"If he was calling the abductor, it would've taken all of thirty seconds for him to give them the information on Coco. Sounds more like he was on hold while ordering pizza."

"Yeah, agree. If he did call a partner that night, he didn't use his personal cell." Mila stretched out her legs and folded her arms. "Torres is coming in at nine?"

"That's what he said."

Mila checked her Fitbit. They still had an hour. Leaning forward, she wiggled her mouse and brought her screen to life. Then she pulled up Facebook and searched for Roberto Torres. After scrolling through a few pages of Torreses, she finally found his. It was pretty scarce. Nothing updated in the last year. There were some photos of him on a boat two years ago with two other men. She didn't recognize them, and they weren't tagged. No photos at the Seafood Festival. Nothing that would indicate he knew Forester. She moved on to the other social media sites and then just Googled his name.

"Hey, I think I got something." Aiden whirled around in his chair and handed her two bank statements. "Check out the deposit I highlighted."

Mila scanned the sheet, her eyes zeroing in on the two-thousand-dollar cash deposit and then over to the date. "A week before Coco disappeared." She met Aiden's gaze. "This fits the theory that someone paid him to let them know when a little girl was left alone."

"Yep." Aiden ran a hand roughly over his face. "And what better person to bribe than someone who has access to the school and little girls?"

Mila's mouth twisted in thought. "How do you want to approach Torres with this information?"

Aiden shook his head. "He's going to know he's a suspect as soon as we tell him we've pulled his financials. We have to keep it friendly."

Aiden's desk phone rang. He scooted forward and plucked up the receiver. "Detective Reyes."

As he listened, he turned back toward Mila, his jaw twitching. He shook his head slowly. "Mr. Torres, I understand your concern, but I assure you we just need your help with a few more details." His eyes squeezed shut and his nostrils flared.

Mila's stomach sank.

"Sure. Okay, have a good evening."

"He's not coming in, is he?" she asked.

Aiden shook his head. "His sister called him and told him to get a lawyer. The lawyer told him not to come in and answer questions voluntarily."

"Shit." Mila bit the inside of her cheek, thinking. "His *sister* called him? Or did Roman Forester call him?"

Aiden glanced up sharply. "How would Forester know we were talking to him?"

"He showed up at my house yesterday, and I asked him if he knew Torres."

A flash of anger darkened Aiden's expression. "Forester showed up at your house? That sounds like a threat."

She shrugged. "It's hard to say. He was friendly enough."

Aiden's brows pressed down in concern. "And he denied knowing Torres?"

"Of course."

"Damn it." Aiden yanked off his tie and unbuttoned his dress shirt. "All right, let's go back further in Torres's phone logs and see if we can find any connection to Forester."

Around ten that night, after an exhausting search of Torres's phone records which turned up nothing, Mila drove to Logan's house and pulled up next to his truck in the driveway. Good, he was home. She hadn't been able to get that Texas article out of her head all day.

He answered the door in a pair of gym shorts, a gray T-shirt, and a five o'clock shadow.

"Hey." His gaze swept over her face as he moved aside to let her in. He shut the door, still holding her stare, then stepped forward and ran the back of his hand down her cheek. "Tough day?"

Mila shivered despite herself. "You could say that."

"Need a drink?" he asked, closing the gap between them and tilting her chin up with an index finger. "Or something else?" He pressed his lips against hers in a soft questioning kiss. His arm encircled her waist and pulled her body flush against his own.

She moaned as his lips moved to her jaw and peppered kisses along her neck. She needed to talk first. She pressed her palm against his chest. "Drink first."

He chuckled in her ear and gave her neck a sharp bite before letting her go and moving into the kitchen.

She plopped down on the sofa, willing her body to stand down. Country music was playing low as usual. A laptop and some files were spread out on the coffee table. He obviously brought his work home.

He returned and handed her a tumbler full of scotch, then took a seat next to her and squeezed her thigh. "So, no progress today, I take it?"

She let herself enjoy the warmth of his hand through her slacks and the burn of the scotch warming her throat and then shook her head. "No. But I did find something I wanted to talk to you about."

His hand massaged her thigh as he flicked his eyes up to hers. "Okay."

She held his gaze so she wouldn't miss his reaction. "I came across an article today about a little girl who died on her sixth birthday in Texas. Her name was Magnolia Scott. Any relation?"

Logan's hand froze on her leg and his face drained of color. He squeezed his eyes shut and then blew out a deep breath, his head beginning to nod. "She was my little sister." When he opened his eyes, they were black with pain, guilt and sorrow. His voice was a hoarse whisper. "It's why Amelia's case has me so fucked up. I couldn't save her, either."

She rested her hand on top of his and felt it trembling. "Why didn't you say anything?"

"I've never told anyone. I... just... can't talk about it."

Mila steeled herself against the guilt as she said, "Please don't take this the wrong way. You know I have to chase every lead on this case. That theory you had about someone taking these two girls to protect them? It's a good one. And it would have had to have been someone who knew both girls, or at least knew about both of them being put in danger by their parents. A cop with access to arrest records would know that."

Logan was listening quietly, sadness pooling in his eyes.

She softened her voice as she continued. "You have a reason to protect two six-year-old little girls, and you have a drone, Logan." She gave him a meaningful look.

He blinked a few times and then he said, "I see." His thumb began to rub circles on her thigh as he thought for a moment.

"You understand I have to rule you out as a suspect, right?" Mila hated the look on his face, but finding Coco was her top priority.

He met her gaze. His eyes were glassy with pain, but to his credit, he didn't react with anger. "Of course. What do you need?"

She thought for a moment. "Is there a shed or other structure on this property?"

"Yes."

"I need you to show it to me."

With a pinched smile, he slowly stood from the sofa and took her hand. "Come on."

Grabbing a set of keys off the bar, he flipped on an outside light. He released her hand so he could slide open the glass doors that led to a screened lanai and stepped outside.

She touched her Glock for comfort, watching his face carefully in case this was a trap. She hated thinking that about him. He'd done nothing but help her with this case. But she'd learned to put safety above all else. Especially feelings. She stayed back a few feet as she followed him.

He led her silently through the lanai screened door and out to the backyard. He didn't look back at her once. She was grateful for that. She didn't want to see the hurt in his eyes again.

She followed him down a stone path through the large backyard caged in by a black wrought iron fence. Oak trees, palmetto bushes and thick brush surrounded the yard, creating a second barrier. It was a nice piece of property that still had that old Florida feel.

As he stopped in front of a large wooden shed in the back corner shadows, a symphony of frogs croaking and nightbird songs filled the silence between them.

She stood back a few feet, her body tense as he slid a key into the padlock and removed it. Without glancing back at her, he opened the door and stepped aside.

Mila pulled her phone out and turned on the flashlight. Sweeping the light across a riding lawnmower and various other yard tools, she breathed a sigh of relief. Nodding, she stepped inside and looked around, making sure she wasn't missing something big like a body.

"Thank you," she said sheepishly, stepping back out and letting him slide the lock back on.

He turned and pulled her into him, whispering in her ear, "I understand."

Slipping her arms around his waist, she pressed her ear against his chest and listened to the slow, steady beat of his heart. "And I'm sorry about your little sister."

She felt too guilty for suspecting him to stay. Instead, she kissed him, letting her body say everything she couldn't, and then left to grab a few hours of sleep in her own bed.

Nineteen

When she arrived at the station in the morning, there was a buzz of activity. She pushed her way through the crowd of uniforms to where Captain Bartol was standing with Aiden.

"What's going on?" Mila asked.

"Forester has agreed to let us search his mansion." She motioned to the group of uniforms around her. "They're about ready to head over."

"Holy shit," Mila whispered. "Are we sure that's a good idea? I mean, if we're getting close to finding anything, he could just stop us."

Captain Bartol sighed. "We're not getting a warrant anytime soon."

Aiden shot her a hopeful look. "Ride with me?"

This was a bad idea, but they were out of good ones. "Okay. Let's go."

Billowy white clouds filled the sky above the mansion, and the temperature had already reached the mid-eighties, as the convoy of police cars filed through Forester's front gate. They pulled around the fountain and parked, engines clicking in the silence. Mila and Aiden were right behind them.

The officers exited their cars, eyes nervously searching the grounds, their jaws tight as they waited for the detectives to serve the warrant.

Forester stepped out through the doors, hands shoved in the pockets of white cotton pants, a patient smile plastered on his face.

Mila studied him as his gaze roamed over the circus his property had become.

Relaxed. Amused.

"She's not going to be here. Not if he's letting us search," she said to Aiden.

"No, but there may be some evidence left behind even if he... moved her."

Mila cringed. She heard the unspoken words.

Killed her. Disposed of her.

They exited the car and walked up the half-moon stone steps to stand in front of Forester.

Mila looked him over as she said, "Good morning."

Aiden held out a clipboard and pen. "Morning, Mr. Forester. This is stating you're giving your consent to a search of this property."

His gray eyes sparkled in the morning light as he smiled at Mila. He scribbled his name on the form and handed it back to Aiden. "Good morning, detectives. I hope my cooperation will help you move on to find the rightful monster."

Mila shifted on her feet. She was torn between suspicion and feeling like she owed him some gratitude for letting them conduct a search. She decided gratitude would go further. "We appreciate your cooperation. Is your mother inside?"

He rocked back on his heels. "No. Ms. Vanore has taken her out for breakfast. She doesn't need the stress."

Mila nodded and then noticed the uniforms moving down the driveway toward them in a line. She counted twelve officers and two forensic techs. She gave them the go-ahead.

"We'll be out of your hair as soon as possible." She moved back down the steps and grabbed one of the techs. "Make sure to collect any hair from the shower and bath drains. And there's a Rolls Royce in the garage. Pay special attention to it, hair, blood, fibers, prints."

The tech nodded her understanding.

Mila and Aiden stepped inside behind the officers and watched them fan out into the cavernous house.

"I'm going upstairs," she said, her heartbeat picking up. This is what she'd wanted to do since her first visit here. She wasn't going to waste any time.

The top of the stairs branched off into two hallways. She turned left and started with the opened French doors at the end of the hall. Stepping into the room, she knew immediately this was Roman's bedroom. Thick white carpeting, violet. pink and gold décor, a chandelier over the four-poster bed, and huge paintings of young girls hung on every wall.

She slipped on gloves and moved deeper into the room. He wouldn't have kept Coco in here, but there may be other evidence. The ratty clothes he wore, the drone.

She crossed the room and into a walk-in closet that was the size of her whole bedroom. A light flickered on automatically. She took in the vast array of clothes. Some button-down shirts, suits, slacks but also a ton of dresses, sparkly costumes, rows and rows of high-heeled shoes, purses, and wigs.

She dug around in the back of the closet, looking for any sign of the hoodie and jeans the kidnapper was wearing. She opened boxes, pulled out drawers, even went through his dirty laundry basket. *Nothing.* Of course, he wouldn't be careless enough to keep such a large piece of evidence against him such as those clothes.

She stood with her fists planted on her hips, thinking and letting her gaze roam over the wigs, something tickling at her consciousness. Something trying to nudge her. As she heard officers enter the bedroom, she turned on her heels and went to check out the other rooms on the floor.

There was his mother's room, which was as large as Roman's, with an ensuite bathroom, plus an office, and six bedrooms. Most of them were generically decorated, but as Mila stepped into the last one, a chill raced up her spine.

It was a playroom. A playroom for little girls.

Dolls of every size sat on custom shelves. A round table in the middle of the room held a China tea set and plastic fruit, cupcakes and various other sweets. Stuffed animals sat in the chairs waiting to be served.

And on the back wall was a glass case full of sparkling princess crowns.

Her head drained of blood, and she had to grab the doorframe as a wave of dizziness swept over her. Backing out of the room, she went to find one of the forensic techs and brought her to the room.

"I want everything in here photographed, fingerprinted and swabbed." There was no way Roman could get rid of every print or bit of DNA if Coco had been in this room.

Have we just caught our break?

Three hours later, the search was complete, and they headed back to the station. Coco hadn't been there, but maybe their first big break had been.

"I've asked the FDLE to help process some of the evidence and put a rush on it," Captain Bartol said, obvious hope shining in her eyes. "And we'll have units sitting on Forester until results come in. He's definitely a flight risk."

Mila sat at her desk, looking over her notes. Searching Forester's place had to bring them closer to an answer, closer to bringing Coco home. She wanted to call Raelynn and give her an update on the investigation, but false hope wouldn't be helpful. No, she'd call her when they had something solid.

Her mind wandered back to Logan. How much damage had losing his little sister done to him? To his parents?

She realized now that it was his darkness, his pain that she had felt the kinship with. It also explained the deep-seated guilt she'd noticed from the beginning. Not being able to save his little sister and then not being able to find and save Amelia. She would be devastated, too.

With a sigh she returned to her notes, trying to figure out her next move. They still had to figure out if Torres was involved somehow.

She spent the day making calls and setting up interviews.

When five o'clock rolled around, she decided to take a break and go home to have dinner with Harper and Kittie. As they caught up over chicken carbonara, Mila's mind kept wandering back to motive. That was the one thing she couldn't figure out. No sexual assault. Why keep Amelia for three years then? She chewed the soft pasta and smiled at Harper, as she told a story about an armadillo on their playground today, but her thoughts were being poked by a sharp stick named Logan Scott.

The problem was, since learning about his sister's death, she couldn't deny the fact that he had motive. And it was a motive he suggested. Taking those girls to protect them from a dangerous home environment. But then again, she couldn't see him hurting Amelia if that was the case, let alone killing her.

The devil on her shoulder whispered that he could've had opportunity. She had no idea where he was when either girl was taken. The only thing he didn't have was means. No boat to dump the body. Well, no boat that she knew of. His name wasn't on the list of boat rentals. But did he own one? There wasn't one at his house. Could he be keeping it in storage somewhere? If she could be sure he didn't have a boat, she could stop worrying that she was letting her personal feelings get in the way of the case.

When she returned to work, she made a beeline for Frank's desk. "Hey, Frank, you have that FDLE list of boats registered in their area?"

"Yeah, somewhere." He began to dig through the piles on his desk. He glanced up at her. "You got something?"

"God, I hope not," she whispered under her breath. "Just double checking something."

"Ah," he held up a packet of stapled papers. "Here ya go."

Her lower back began to cramp as she sat at her desk and scanned page after page. Jesus, there were a lot of boats in Edgewater.

Suddenly she sat up. A rush of heat flushed her body.

Logan's name was on the list. He owned a 2019 Mako 18 LTS.

Where did he keep it?

She stared at her monitor, thinking about his property. About the woods surrounding it. Could it be hidden beyond his fence in those woods? With a mixture of disbelief and dread, she pulled up Google Maps and searched for his address.

When she clicked on the photo layer, she could see what she had missed.

Damn it. Sloppy, Mila.

The yard was there and the shed he'd let her search, but the woods stretched further back than she could see from the vantage point of the backyard. His property ended at a canal. There was another structure. Another shed, maybe? And a dock.

She zoomed out and followed the canal. It fed into old Tampa Bay. And if he had a boat, all he would've had to do to get to Rattlesnake Island was go around the tip of Ft. Desoto Park and cruise up the coast a few miles.

She bit her lip. *Is this what the job has done to her? Made her so paranoid that she's suspecting one of their own?* And not just another cop, but a man who'd worked with her side by side to solve these cases, and a man she'd shared a bed with. Just by this accusation alone, she could ruin his career. Not to mention his mental health since he's already suffering from so much guilt and pain.

"What's up?" Aiden stopped next to her with a cup of steaming noodles. "You look deep in thought. Anything I can help with?"

No, she had to be sure before she ruined his life. After a few beats, she grabbed her bag. "I need to go check out something." She looked at her Fitbit. It was almost eight o'clock. She met Aiden's curious stare. "If I don't call you in two hours, check my GPS and come find me."

Twenty

Mila parked down the street, out of sight, and turned off her running lights in case Logan happened to look out his window. She grabbed her flashlight, touched her holster for comfort, and quietly stalked into the brush beside his house. She didn't dare turn on the flashlight until she was sure he couldn't see the light from his bedroom window, so her progress was slow as she navigated the underbrush. She kept to the edge, with just a few feet of brush between her and his wrought iron fence as a guide. When she was sure she had the cover of the shed at her back, she flicked on the flashlight and then moved deeper into the woods.

If he was using the dock she saw on Google Maps, there had to be a path to it.

Something rustled to her left and she paused, listening. The noise came again, but it was from a small creature. Armadillo or snake probably. She pushed on, feeling the pointing palmetto bushes stab her through her slacks as sweat trickled down her spine. With a silent curse, she slapped at something that landed on her neck.

Finally, she broke out into a small clearing. Glancing back, she couldn't see the house, so she swept the flashlight over the brush in front of her. There it was. A narrow path cutting through the brush. It must lead to the canal and dock.

From there, it was much easier to make her way toward the back of the property as she kept her flashlight trained on the path. After about a five-minute trek, she stepped out of the woods and froze, taking in what was in front of her. A wide canal, its waters calm and dark.

On her side of the canal sat a nineteen-foot white bay boat tied to a squat, wooden dock. A 10'x12' shed painted dark blue sat on her right. On the opposite bank was more wild brush and trees. No homes. No one to hear a little girl's cries.

Why wouldn't he show her this when she'd asked? There was only one reason she could think of. But it couldn't be right. *Denial. Shock. Suspicion.* They all swirled inside her like a gathering storm as she carefully moved closer to the double doors of the shed.

There were no windows, but light seeped through a crack at the bottom.

Why would he hook up electricity to a shed? Again, only one reason came to mind.

Her stomach clenched. This was bad.

She shone her flashlight on the padlock holding the doors closed. *Damn.* She had bolt cutters back in her SUV. She'd have to go back for them.

Another noise behind her startled her. It was louder this time.

A crunch and a swish of movement.

She slipped to the side of the shed and pressed her body against it, trying to slow down her breathing. She waited. As the seconds ticked painfully by, she only heard the croaks and chirps of frogs and insects.

Wait. Was that footsteps?

Yes.

Someone was coming. She strained to listen as the footsteps came closer.

Then keys rattled and the padlock thunked on the ground.

Mila pressed herself tighter against the shed wall. Her pulse thumped in her ears.

The doors squeaked open, and she heard Logan's gentle voice on the other side of the wall where her head rested. "I brought you some ice cream."

"Thank you," a little girl's voice replied back.

No. no. no.

Shock flooded her brain. *How could this be?* Confusion and then horror and then betrayal all piled up against her psyche. All this time, he'd been acting like he was helping her, like he cared if Coco was found safe… all this time he was the one who took her.

How did she miss this?

You can beat yourself up later. Coco still isn't safe.

She sucked a deep breath into her lungs and forced herself to push aside all feelings and questions. It was time to do her job.

Slowly, she crept back around the edge of the shed, unsnapping the strap on her holster with her thumb and pulling out her Glock. She would have to be careful she didn't give Logan an opportunity to use Coco as a shield. She shook her head, still in disbelief that the man she'd gotten to know and care about was the man she was about to confront.

Soft light poured out of the small structure now. She leaned forward to take in the scene. There was a single bed, toys and Barbies spread out on the floor, a lamp, and a small refrigerator. An air conditioning unit mounted in the wall hummed loudly.

Logan sat on the bed in jeans and a white T-shirt.

Coco sat cross-legged beside him, jamming a spoon into a container of Ben & Jerry's ice cream. She was wearing a purple tutu and a plastic ruby necklace over her shorts and T-shirt, curly hair wild and unbrushed.

The relief of seeing the little girl alive almost brought Mila to her knees. She pulled back and blinked away the tears suddenly blurring her vision. She was grateful for the air conditioning unit noise, otherwise he'd probably hear her heart pounding in her chest.

She quietly moved back around to the side of the shed and reached for her phone. *Damn.* It was still in the SUV. She had to get Logan away from Coco. Maybe she should wait until he returned to the house? Then she could go back to her SUV and call for backup.

Coco's sobs suddenly cut through the night sounds. Mila heard them talking but couldn't make out what they were saying. She had to know if Coco was in immediate danger, so she slid back around to the front of the shed.

"When can I go home? I miss Mommy."

"I know. But we have to make sure Mommy understands that she needs to do a better job of keeping you safe. She forgot that. So, we're just reminding her. Just think of this like a vacation."

Coco's sobs deepened.

And then Mila remembered Amelia Larson.

Had he taken her, too? And killed her? Was he lying to Coco about letting her go home? Is this the wound she knew lay beneath his darkness?

Mila felt a rush of rage so powerful, it threatened to catapult her forward and put a bullet into Logan. How could he do this? He was a fucking cop. He swore an oath. And she had trusted him. Let him in.

All she could hear was the blood rushing into her ears as she lifted her Glock and swung her body around to fill the doorway.

Unfortunately, Logan must have heard or sensed something. He was standing right there. She gasped as their eyes clashed.

He took advantage of her surprise, his palms shooting out, the right one grasping her wrist, the left one expertly twisting the Glock from her hand. Luckily her finger wasn't on the trigger, or it would've snapped like a twig under his force.

Mila stumbled back a few steps as Coco screamed. Her breathing grew erratic. Her vision became a tunnel focused on the gun now in Logan's hand.

It registered that he held the gun to his side, not pointing at her. That was something.

She held her hands up slowly and raised her gaze to his face.

His eyes were shining with regret, the mask gone and the darkness within him on full display. "Mila," he moaned. The agony in his voice matched the tension in his body. "I'm so sorry."

Mila glanced behind him. Coco had pressed herself against the wall. She was crying into a stuffed bear, clutching it like a shield in front of her body. She looked so small. So scared.

"Let's just talk," Mila said quietly. She took another step back, hoping she could pull him out of the shed, put some distance between him and Coco. "I heard you, Logan. I know you're just protecting Coco from a mother who was reckless with her safety. I know you were going to let her go home once Raelynn learned her lesson. I'll testify to that."

He held her gaze. "And Amelia?" he whispered hoarsely. "What will you say about her? She didn't make it home."

So, he did take Amelia, too. Mila dropped her hands but watched every twitch he made, every change in expression carefully. "Why? What happened, Logan? I know you didn't want to hurt her." She took another step back, and it had the desired effect.

Logan took three strides forward bringing him out of the shed. But now he tapped her Glock lightly on the side of his leg, his other hand scrubbing his face roughly. He looked like a man on the edge of despair. With nothing to lose.

Mila felt an unnatural calmness take over. Her voice was steady as she said, "Hey, it's me. Talk to me, Logan. Tell me what happened."

His shoulders fell but his dark eyes stayed locked on hers. "I did take her, but I didn't kill her... Amelia. I want you to know that." His tone was now void of emotion. "Not on purpose anyway. It happened the night of the hurricane. The power went out. I think she got scared and climbed into an old cedar chest I'd put in there for her toys. It locked. I was stuck at the station until the next morning. By the time I got here, she'd suffocated." His voice broke, and his expression shattered.

Christ. Just an accident. An accident that wouldn't have happened if he hadn't taken her, though.

She heard the regret in her own voice as she asked, "Why did you keep her for so long?"

His head swung slowly back and forth like he was trying to figure out the same thing. "When I decided to take her, it was just to scare Amelia's mother into being more careful who she let around her kid. A few inches over and that bullet could've ended her life. Didn't she realize what a precious gift she had?" His expression tightened in agony. "My parents would give anything to have their baby girl back with them." Then his mouth opened and closed like he was having trouble finding the words. When he finally pushed them out, Mila had to strain to hear him. "But then I realized how nice it was having her around. Honestly, I was selfish. It felt like I had a second chance at having a little sister."

"Magnolia," Mila offered.

At her name, a sound of grief tore from his chest, a cross between a moan and roar. "That... her death.... that *was* my fault. I suppose my parents deserve the truth. That day she was following me around, and I was climbing the tree to get away from her. I just got so annoyed when she tried to follow me, I kicked out at her beneath me. I didn't mean to hurt her.

It was just one second of anger. One goddamn second that ended her life, changed the course of ours. Destroyed our family. On her birthday." He choked on his next words. "It took one second to change a boy into a monster."

Mila watched his chest rapidly rise and fall. She didn't know how he was still standing under the weight of that guilt. Maybe he wasn't, though. Not mentally, anyway. Kidnapping a child to keep her safe sounds like some sort of psychotic break to her. "That's why you left the birthday crown with Amelia?"

Tears glistened on his cheeks now. He swiped at them with the hand that held the gun. He was getting reckless. "Yeah. It was the one thing I'd kept of Magnolia's. To remind me of what I'd done. Amelia liked to wear it, so it was the last thing I could give her." A groan escaped his throat. "She was such a sweet girl. I can't believe I..." His words faded as a look of horror flickered over his face. His gaze suddenly seemed unfocused, looking through her instead of at her.

Mila took a tiny step forward, testing how much he was paying attention. His eyes snapped back to her. She needed to keep him talking. "But you did try to make it look like Forester took Coco. Why?"

"He's a creep. His obsession with little girls is unnatural." He shifted on his feet, his expression hardening. "Besides, it was easy enough with a wig and a fake limp. I knew there was a camera trained on the playground and park trail, and I had to throw suspicion onto someone else."

"And what about Roberto Torres? You added the handwritten note in the files about him not cooperating, didn't you?" She took another tiny shuffle forward. She was still aware of Coco's soft cries in the background, but all her focus was on getting the gun out of Logan's hands.

He nodded. "I just needed to buy some time. I was only going to keep Coco for a few more days. Then I figured the pressure would be off of the investigation, she could go home, and it could go unsolved like Amelia's. But you're good, Mila. I wish you weren't."

Mila remembered the hooded man across from her mom's coffee shop. "Did you follow me, too? Try to scare me into backing off?"

His brows pressed down, and he shook his head. "No." Then his whole demeanor shifted, softened. "I am glad I met you, though."

She didn't like the finality in his tone. She had to force this into a confrontation she could control. Get the gun closer to her so she could disarm him. Gritting her teeth, she moved quickly a few steps toward him.

On reflex, as she expected, he lifted the Glock to point it at her.

Muscle memory kicked in. Both her hands shot up together as her head lowered out of the way. As her palms pushed the Glock skyward, it went off. With the boom still ringing in her ears, her right foot shot out and connected with his groin.

"Oof," he grunted in pain.

Mila's left foot stepped into him, knocking him off balance.

She'd meant to twist the Glock out of his hand and step back with it, but he grabbed her arm and brought her down with him as he fell backward.

The Glock bounced and landed somewhere in the grass.

As soon as they hit the ground, Logan rolled them over and straddled her. He immediately pinned her hands on the ground above her head. His chest was heaving, breath coming in hard pants.

The dampness soaked through her shirt, and he was pressing her arm into a sharp stone.

"Mila, stop," he whispered harshly. "I don't want to hurt you."

"Don't worry. You won't." She bucked her hips upward, forcing him to angle forward. As soon as his head cleared hers, she whipped her arms down, like she was making a snow angel, breaking his hold. She turned her face so he didn't land on her nose when he fell.

With a groan, he faceplanted in the damp grass.

She immediately wrapped her arms around his torso and pressed herself tight, not giving him any room to attack her again.

"Coco, run!" she yelled. "Run and hide!"

Gripping Logan's body tight, she shimmied herself upward until she could grab one of the arms he was bracing himself with. She yanked it from beneath him, then rolled on top of him. Grabbing his wrist in one hand and his elbow in the other, she pressed and twisted his arm painfully to subdue him.

She caught a rustling sound and a flash of Coco running past them, her sobs filling the thick night air, but she didn't dare take her attention off Logan. "It's over."

Even as he grimaced in pain from the pressure she was exerting on his shoulder and elbow joints, he was struggling beneath her.

Her muscles were shaking with adrenaline and fatigue. She could kick herself for not bringing handcuffs. She needed her Glock if she was going to get him to cooperate. Knowing it was risky, she pulled her attention off him and scanned the grass for her weapon. She spotted it a few feet away, but the move cost her.

Logan took advantage of the moment of distraction to buck and roll her off him. He must've noticed where her gaze landed because he immediately pushed up and dove for the weapon.

Mila's legs shook as she tried and failed to get up fast enough to disarm him again.

They locked eyes and rose to their feet at the same time, about ten feet apart. They were both panting hard.

Mila's gut clenched as he held the gun up to his temple and placed his finger on the trigger. She could see in his eyes, in the defeat and despair swirling in them, that he wasn't bluffing. His decision was made.

She held up her palms and tried to calm her breathing. "Logan, you don't want to do this. Taking another life isn't the answer here." She took a tentative step forward.

"Stop." He pressed the gun harder into his temple. "It's what I deserve, Mila. It's what Amelia Larson's mom deserves. What my parents deserve. Justice." A final smile touched his lips. "Thank you for making me feel something other than guilt and pain for the first time since I was ten. I hope you have a good life."

The crack of the gunshot echoed in the night air and rang in her ears.

Mila screamed and lurched forward as his body seemed frozen for a second before it collapsed on the ground.

She fell to her knees beside him and grabbed his warm hand. "No, no, no. Why did you do this>" Her body went numb, and a buzzing started in her brain as she let herself look at his face, at the blood seeping into the grass, at the light gone from his eyes.

She had failed him.

This man who she had thought she may be able to open up to, who she had shared late-night drinks, theories, and intimate moments in his bed. He was gone.

"I'm so sorry," she choked out.

She released his hand. The body that had given her pleasure for the first time in years now belonged to the medical examiner.

She couldn't think about that now. Swiping at the sweat and tears on her face, she pushed herself up and turned her attention to the woods.

"Coco!" she shouted. Moving quickly back down the path, she yelled for the little girl until her throat was raw but got no response.

Where is she?

Twenty-One

Back at her SUV, she called dispatch and then Captain Bartol, explained the situation and gave them all Logan's address. Then, making sure she had her phone this time, she rushed back into the brush to continue the search for Coco.

Finding a narrow path forged by wild boars, she made better time and covered more ground as she swept her flashlight over and under the brush.

"Coco!" she called out. "It's safe to come out now."

Within ten minutes, she heard the sirens and headed back toward the street. Emerging from the woods, she waved down the first squad car, a Crystal Harbor PD unit. Two officers flung open their doors and quickly approached her.

"Riley," the red-headed male officer held out his hand.

Mila shook it, and then the young female officer's, before getting down to business. "We've got a missing six-year-old girl, Coco Parks, in these woods somewhere."

The female officer pulled out her flashlight. "Thank God she's alive." She nodded at her partner. "Let's go find her."

Mila walked over and grabbed a warm water bottle from her SUV console and took a few swallows. Her shirt was plastered to her body with sweat, her body weak from the earlier adrenaline dump.

As she was preparing to resume her search, a firetruck and two more units arrived. The woods were now lit up with swirling red and blue lights. These were Edgewater PD.

She changed direction, and Officers Gentry and Simms met her in the street.

"What do you need?" Simms asked, his expression grim.

"A perimeter set up around the shed and... body." Logan's lifeless eyes flashed in her mind. She forced the image away.

Gentry reached out and squeezed her shoulder. "Show us."

After they grabbed some supplies from their trunk, Mila led them back to the shed via the backyard. Then she once again pushed back into the woods. She'd retrieved her flashlight, so it made it a little easier to see, but the brush was thick, the hiding places many. She made sure to sweep the light beneath every bush. It seemed Coco was too scared to come out of her hiding place.

While deep in the brush, she could hear more sirens approaching. Maybe Coco would hear those, too, and head toward the sound. She thought about the canal and her breath seized in her chest. What if Coco had fallen in? It was dark out. She could have misstepped.

"Coco!" she screamed louder, joining the other voices calling for the girl in the distance.

Her phone buzzed in her pocket. She pulled it out, almost dropping it as her palm was slick with sweat. *Aiden.* "What's up?"

"I picked up Raelynn. We're about five minutes out. Find her yet?"

"Not yet. Think you could get one of those CART dogs out here quickly?"

"Sure. I'll call the captain."

She changed course, making her way back to the shed. Gentry and Simms were still busy cordoning off the whole area with crime scene tape. They had already put up a separate barrier around Logan's body. She forced herself not to look as she grabbed the stuffed bear Coco had been clutching for the scent dog.

She jogged back down the path, threw open the gate that led to Logan's backyard and hurried out to the road.

The street in front of Logan's house was now packed with police cruisers, an ambulance, a firetruck and an ME crime scene van. There was a flurry of activity with radios squawking, people shouting, and coming in and out of the woods.

She spotted Captain Bartol standing with the CART leader and two men she didn't recognize.

"Mila." Captain Bartol's worried gaze swept over Mila as she approached. "Are you okay? Do you need medical attention?"

"I'm fine." She handed the stuffed bear over. "This has Coco's scent."

"Okay, good. The dog will be here in five." She waved P.J. O'Malley and Rhodes over. They greeted Mila with somber expressions. "Take them back to the shed to start processing."

"We'll go through the backyard, easier access," she told them. As she turned to go, she caught Aiden and Raelynn rushing toward her. "Give me one sec."

When they reached her, Raelynn grabbed Mila's arms, desperation and hope waring in her eyes. Her face was gaunt, her hair greasy. "Did you find her?"

Mila was careful to keep her expression neutral, and not show the frustration she was feeling. "We will. I told her to hide, so that's what she's doing but she's safe now. There's a scent dog that will be here any minute." She extracted Raelynn's ice-cold fingers from her arms and squeezed them. "We'll find her." She met Aiden's eyes and nodded.

He gripped Raelynn's shoulders. "Come on, let's stay out of the way. We'll wait over here."

Mila turned and motioned to P.J. O'Malley and Rhodes that she was ready. She led them back through the yard, down the path through the woods and out to the shed by the canal.

"This is where he was holding Coco." Her voice was raspy from yelling for the little girl.

"Jesus, a cop. Guess you never really know someone," P.J. whispered, then shook her head and ducked under the yellow tape.

Mila turned away, ready to give her effort back to the search.

Okay, where are you, Coco?

She rested her hands on her hips and stared into the shadowy brush. Only a sliver of moon hung in sky. There wasn't enough light to get through the brush without a flashlight, which Coco didn't have. Where would she go to feel safe if she were a child? Where would Harper go?

Suddenly her breath hitched in her chest. Her eyes widened.

It damn sure wouldn't be in the dark woods.

Her gut told her she was right.

She pushed her way out of the woods back into the yard, a new sense of urgency doubling her pulse. She checked the shed in the backyard first. Locked. Then she jogged down the stone path, entered the lanai, and stared at the sliding glass doors that led inside the house.

One was cracked open.

Sliding it open farther, she stepped inside, straining to hear any sound. Her gaze swept over the kitchen to her right. The light above the stove was on. There was a plate and a glass on the counter. Shoving aside the sudden flash of memory of her and Logan's first kiss, she crept into the living room. The radio was on as usual. A heartbreaking country song. Appropriate.

Mila squeezed her eyes shut for a second as a stab of pain hit her in the heart. No matter what he'd done, she had grown to care about him. He was just here, enjoying a meal, listening to this music. And now he's gone forever.

Stop.

She forced herself back to what was important. There would be time later to untangle her feelings about Logan.

"Coco? It's Detective Harlow. You're safe now. Your mom is waiting for you outside." She cocked her head and then spun around toward the hallway bathroom as a small sniffling noise came from that direction. Taking a few steps forward, she concentrated, listening for more sounds. Yeah, definitely sniffling. "Do you want to see your mom, sweetie?"

Coco's small face peered out at her from the bathroom door, round, dark eyes glistening with tears.

Mila blew out a breath and felt faint with relief. She lowered herself to her knees and held out her arms. "The bad man is gone. You're safe now."

With a cry, Coco rushed down the hall and flung herself into Mila's arms. Her tiny hands pressed into the back of Mila's neck as she sobbed and hiccupped and shook. She was still wearing the tutu and plastic necklace. Her feet were bare, and Mila was sure she'd find cuts on the bottoms of them, but she'd let the medics worry about that. Right now, she just held her.

Mila had to blink back her own tears as she patted the little girl's back and gave her time to process feeling safe.

After a few moments, Coco pulled back and stared up into Mila's face. Snot and tears were shiny on her full cheeks. "Can I see my mommy now?"

Mila smiled. "Of course. Let's go." She lifted the girl, so light and small and warm, into her arms and carried her out the front door.

She stepped out onto the porch. Glancing around the chaotic scene of people and flashing lights, she finally spotted Aiden and Raelynn talking to Captain Bartol and headed that way.

"Mommy!" Coco sobbed as she turned her head and caught sight of her mother. Her little body twisted in Mila's arms, trying to keep her mom in view.

Raelynn's head jerked up at the sound, and her hands flew to her mouth. She took a few stumbling steps forward.

Aiden caught her and held her upright as Mila brought her daughter back to her.

"Oh my God," Raelynn breathed as Coco reached for her, and Raelynn pulled her out of Mila's arms. "My baby," she choked. She held her against her chest, her lips pressed into the top of her head as they both sobbed.

A murmuring crowd pushed forward and surrounded them, but Mila couldn't pull her gaze away from Coco safe in her mother's arms. It was over. It was finally over. Coco was found alive. They had got their miracle.

Two EMTs took over, pushing through the crowd and leading the shaken mom and daughter to the back of the ambulance. Coco would need to go to the hospital to get checked out.

Suddenly there was a commotion behind the patrol cars lined up on the street.

Mila and Aiden shared a concerned glance and then headed that way.

Captain Bartol had her hands on her hips, never a good sign, and was watching as four uniformed officers stood in a line.

"You have no right to keep this from the people," an angry voice yelled.

Mila's eyes narrowed. She knew that voice. Elly Prescott. "How did she get here so fast?" she wondered out loud.

The officers forced Elly and her cameraman farther down the street, away from Raelynn and Coco, and back behind the crime scene barrier they had set up. There were about a dozen onlookers already pressed up against it.

Captain Bartol turned with a scowl and stomped back to the ambulance.

"Mila!" someone called.

Mila turned and watched Paul trotting toward her. She crossed her arms, her stomach clenching.

He reached her and pulled her into his arms. When she didn't uncross her arms, he released her and looked into her eyes. "You okay?"

She glared at him. "Did you bring her here?"

His eyes filled with confusion. "Who?"

She jerked her head, motioning behind her. "Your girlfriend."

"I don't..." he shook his head. Then they both heard Elly yelling. "Oh."

Mila watched as his expression morphed from confusion to frustration.

His brows were pinched together, and his nostrils flared. "No. She got here on her own. I was with her when she got the call from whoever's been leaking her information. I overheard her side of the conversation."

Mila's shoulders relaxed. He was telling the truth.

"I'm fine," she said, finally answering his question. Though that was a lie. Every muscle in her body ached and she just felt empty inside. "How did you get here so quickly?"

He pulled her back into his arms and rested his chin on the top of her head. "Someone called in gunshots. Brad in dispatch texted me to let me know you were involved."

She let herself accept the comfort, wrapping her arms around his waist. "Yeah. Detective Scott got my gun. Shot himself. He's gone."

"Jesus," he whispered. "It was him? He took Coco?"

"And Amelia Larson," she sighed. "Though he didn't mean to kill her. She accidentally suffocated when she got locked in a cedar chest during the hurricane."

He squeezed her tighter and then pulled back so he could look at her face. She lifted her chin and met his gaze as he said, "I know you have to stay for a bit, but I don't have a shift until tomorrow night. I'll be waiting at the house when you get there."

She nodded, knowing the relief she was feeling would be short-lived. But she would take whatever he could offer her. She didn't want to be alone tonight.

TWENTY-TWO

Mila climbed the stairs quietly, replaying everything that had happened tonight on a loop in her head. Coco was home. Or, at least, she would be after she got examined and treated at the hospital. She'd be sleeping in her own bed tonight.

Unlike Logan.

Could she have done something differently? Stopped Logan from shooting himself?

Her gut roiled as the memory of his body falling played over and over in her head. With effort, she forced the horrifying memory away and opened her bedroom door. She knew Paul would be there as promised. His cruiser was parked in the driveway.

Max lifted his head from his place on the floor next to the bed, and his tail thumped on the carpet. Paul was stretched out on his side of the bed on top of the duvet, still in his jeans and T-shirt, one arm flung over his stomach.

She tiptoed into the bathroom and closed the door.

After getting the shower as hot as she could stand, she stripped and stepped beneath the spray, letting everything wash away and dissolve in the steam. Then she broke down. Deep sobs she tried to keep quiet, but they were rising from her chest and choking her. If Paul heard her, he didn't come in.

Eventually, they receded, and she felt empty again. With the last of the hot water, she scrubbed her hair and body with soap and then stepped out.

Wiping the fogged mirror with her palm, she stared at her reflection, into bloodshot green eyes full of fresh pain. She didn't even recognize herself right now. "It's okay to be sad. It's okay to be human. You did the best you could." She repeated it until she believed it. Then moved back into the dark, cool bedroom and tiptoed to her dresser to grab underwear and a fresh T-shirt.

When she climbed onto the bed, Paul was awake. He had turned to watch her. His blue eyes met hers.

"Come here," he whispered, holding out his arm so she could snuggle up against him. Which she gratefully did.

He wrapped his other arm around her as she rested her cheek on his chest. He pressed his lips into her damp hair. "What do you need?"

His words cracked something open inside her. Hot tears gathered beneath her lids as she squeezed her eyes shut. "Just hold me."

He obliged, pulling her closer, molding their bodies together like they had done thousands of times before. A lifetime ago.

After a few minutes, her body relaxed. She let out a shuddering sigh. "Are you sure you don't have somewhere else to be? Someone else to be with." It was a cheap shot, but she needed reassurance that she still mattered to him. That this wasn't just pity.

He stroked her arm with the pad of his thumb. "She passes the time, Mila. That's it. You are family."

Mila closed her eyes, feeling like she could breathe for the first time all night. "You know this would be easier if you were a dick, right?"

His deep chuckle vibrated beneath her ear. "Get some sleep, babe."

Sometime in the night, Mila woke to find Harper snuggled up to her back and Oscar stretched out at the end of the bed, snoring.

Her whole world in one bed. She smiled as she drifted back into a dreamless sleep.

TWENTY-THREE

Three days later Edgewater was still filled with national news crews interviewing anyone they could get to talk. Eventually, they would move on to another sensational story, but until then, Mila had been keeping a low profile.

This morning, she sat in the coroner's office across from Logan's parents. They had come to pack up his house, take his body back to Texas, and bury him next to Magnolia.

"I'm so sorry for your loss," Mila said. She couldn't imagine outliving one child, let alone both.

Logan's mom was bone thin, her gray hair scraped back in a tight bun. The lines on her face told a story of deep grief and a hard life. His dad was more stoic, sitting straight, eyes the same color as Logan's trained on her. But she could see the pain in his stiff shoulders, his downturned mouth.

"You were the last person to talk to him," he said quietly.

Mila didn't answer because it wasn't a question. She waited for the question.

His gaze turned watery. "Did he say why he did it? Why he took those little girls?"

Mila uncrossed her legs and leaned forward. "In his mind, he was protecting them. Saving them from a danger their home life presented. He didn't mean for Amelia Larson to die. She got locked in a cedar chest accidentally during the hurricane and suffocated."

His mother let out a strangled cry and made the sign of the cross over her body. His father reached over and squeezed her hand, but his eyes didn't leave Mila.

"There's something else he wanted you to know," she continued. "He blamed himself for Magnolia's death because she had been following him around, and he had gotten angry. When she tried to follow him up to the treehouse, he kicked out at her. He caused her to fall."

His dad's face went white with shock before his head dropped into his hands.

"So that's why he wouldn't come home," his mother whispered, tears now streaming down her cheeks. "I guess we lost him a long time ago."

※

Mila held Harper's hand as they walked through the Palm Gates Cemetery. It was a perfect Sunday with bright blue skies, and she finally had a day off. She and Harper had spent the day shopping for a present for her best friend, Hannah, who was turning ten and having a big birthday party the next weekend.

Over mall food court pizza, Harper had asked if she could visit Amelia Larson's grave. It was a strange request, but Mila decided to honor it, hoping it would bring some peace or clarity to whatever questions were going on in her young mind. Her therapist appointment was still two weeks away.

Mila had attended Amelia's funeral on Friday, so she knew where the grave was located. When they reached the fresh tombstone with Amelia's name, dates of birth and death, and an angel carved into the stone, Harper released her mother's hand. She kneeled and placed a bouquet of daisies on top of the fresh dirt.

Still kneeling, her small voice carried on the slight breeze and almost broke Mila's heart.

"I'm sorry you don't get to grow up, that you don't get to go to birthday parties anymore, or have ice cream, or hug your mom." She was silent for a moment and then added, "I hope you're in a place that is happy, and you're not scared anymore."

Mila lifted her chin to blink away the tears and froze. About a hundred feet in front of them was a figure leaning against an oak tree, arms crossed. He wore black jeans, a dark hoodie and sunglasses. She could tell by his unnatural stillness that he was watching them.

Is this the same guy who was standing across from her mom's coffee shop?

She automatically moved her hand to her hip but of course she hadn't taken her Glock to the mall. She reached down and grabbed Harper's hand. When she glanced back up, the person was gone.

She scanned the area. No sign of him. Maybe it was just someone out for a walk or visiting a grave. Still, she felt the need to get Harper to a safe place. "Come on, we have to go."

Harper's head jerked up at the stress in her mother's voice. "Mom?"

"It's okay. Just walk." She led them quickly back down the path that wound through the gravestones, glancing back every few feet to make sure there was no one following.

She didn't breathe until she had Harper safely back in the SUV.

Mila reached over and grabbed her Glock from the glove box. "Stay here. Lock the doors. I'll be right back."

Holding the weapon at her side, she retraced her steps back to Amelia's grave. Stopping to listen for any footsteps or voices, she scanned the area. She didn't like how quiet it was. No birds chattering, no insects. Just a slight rustle of palm fronds in the breeze.

There was no direct path to the tree the man had been leaning against, so she wove her way through the gravestones.

When she got to the tall oak, she examined the ground. The short grass didn't allow for any footprints. When she glanced back up, she caught a blur of movement to her left. She pushed off the tree and ran in that direction. Leaping back onto a cement path, she pushed herself faster, her head on swivel for any other motion. Rounding a corner, she almost ran head-first into an elderly couple walking arm in arm. The woman squeaked and threw her hands up.

"Sorry!" Mila tossed the apology behind her but didn't break her stride. In front of her was a smaller parking area. She ran out into the middle of it and inspected the cars. There were only three and they were empty. She stood there catching her breath for a moment.

Then with a growl of frustration, she made her way back through the cemetery to her SUV.

"What happened?" Harper asked as soon as Mila slid into the driver's seat.

Mila forced a smile and squeezed her daughter's knee to comfort her. "It's nothing to worry about. We're safe. Ready to get ice cream?"

"Sure," Harper answered, still eyeing her mom with skepticism and concern.

Mila's gaze swept over the cemetery once more before backing out of the parking lot. The hairs on her arms were still standing up. Even as she forced the thought of the hooded figure from her mind to enjoy the remaining day with her daughter, her body recognized the threat.

It was one she would face again.

www.ingramcontent.com/pod-product-compliance
Lightning Source LLC
Chambersburg PA
CBHW061237210726
48293CB00003B/795